th**e**ashleys

more books by

melissa de la cruz

FICTION

The Ashleys series

The Ashleys

Jealous?

The Au Pairs series

The Au Pairs

Skinny-dipping

Sun-kissed

Crazy Hot

The Blue Bloods series

Blue Bloods

Masquerade

Angels on Sunset Boulevard

Fresh off the Boat

Cat's Meow

NONFICTION

How to Become Famous in Two Weeks or Less

The Fashionista Files:
Adventures in Four-inch Heels
and Faux Pas

Girls Who Like Boys Who Like Boys:
True Tales of Love, Lust, and Friendship
Between Straight Women and Gay Men

melissa de la cruz

the ashleys
birthday
vicious

aladdin mix

NEW YORK   LONDON   TORONTO   SYDNEY

For my mom and my lola,
who always threw the best birthday parties
And for Mike and Mattie

ALADDIN MIX

Simon & Schuster Children's Publishing Division

1230 Avenue of the Americas, New York, NY 10020

Copyright © 2008 by Melissa de la Cruz

All rights reserved, including the right of reproduction in

whole or in part in any form.

ALADDIN PAPERBACKS, ALADDIN MIX, and related logos are

registered trademarks of Simon & Schuster, Inc.

Designed by Karin Paprocki

The text of this book was set in MrsEavesRoman.

Manufactured in the United States of America

First Aladdin MIX edition August 2008

2 4 6 8 10 9 7 5 3 1

Library of Congress Control Number 2008921949

ISBN-13: 978-1-4169-3408-0

ISBN-10: 1-4169-3408-1

"The Haitians need to come to America. But some people are all, 'What about the strain on our resources?' Well, it's like when I had this garden party for my father's birthday, right? I put R.S.V.P. 'cause it was a sit-down dinner. But some people came that, like, did not R.S.V.P., so I was, like, totally buggin'. I had to haul ass to the kitchen, redistribute the food, squish in extra place settings, but by the end of the day, it was like, the more the merrier! And so, if the government could just get to the kitchen, rearrange some things, we could certainly party with the Haitians. And in conclusion, may I please remind you it does not say R.S.V.P. on the Statue of Liberty! Thank you very much."

—Cher, _Clueless_

Go, go, go shawty
It's your birthday
We gon' party like it's yo birthday . . .
—50 Cent, "In Da Club"

1

ASHLEY FINDS OUT WHAT'S BLACK AND WHITE AND GREEN ALL OVER

SHLEY SPENCER SMOOTHED THE SOFT folds of her Proenza Schouler black-and-white-striped skirt, crossed her spray-tanned, power-yoga-toned legs, and told herself everything was going to be okay. Even though it was exactly a month until her Super-Sweet Thirteen, and her mother was only *now* getting around to a meeting with the party planner, everything was going to work out just *fine*.

The planner in question was Mona Mazur, the most chic, imaginative, and—of course—expensive planner on the West Coast; she'd done parties for the children of everyone who was anyone, from the Chadwick triplets (daughters of the famous singing star) to the various adopted multiracial progeny of the movie stars Barton Flick and Organza Belle, not to mention a Super-Duper Seventh in Vegas for a noto-rious magician's little boy. In other words, Mona was worth waiting for (and Ashley and her mother had been waiting for the better part of an hour already), even if meant doing everything at the last minute.

Another reason Ashley had a good feeling about waiting for Mona: Her office had style oozing out of its davenports. Mona's HQ was a pale green Victorian mansion in Nob Hill, with a terraced French-style front garden and a real gaslight glowing outside the front door. Inside, sitting with her mother on a toile-de-Jouy sofa, Ashley couldn't believe her eyes. Everything, from the floor tiles to the furniture to the silk drapes to the plush sheepskin rug under their feet to the embossed wallpaper, was black and white. Even Mona's dogs, two miniature poodles named Dorothy and Draper, matched the theme: Dorothy was snowy white, Draper was a glossy black, and both wore houndstooth collars.

Ashley was glad she had changed out of her uniform after a long, hard day—well, a short, ordinary kind of day, really, if she was completely honest—at Miss Gamble's, the exclusive girls' school where she and her cabal, the Ashleys, ruled the polished-wood halls and reigned over the seventh grade.

She'd chosen her new skirt and a plush black cashmere sweater, deciding at the last moment on a pair of Miu Miu jeweled ballerina flats—black satin with large trapezoid crystals. And now it seemed like fate, or karma, or one of those hippie things that her father liked to muse about after he came back from yet another ashram, that her clothes reflected the party planner's living-room color scheme. It was inevitable: Ashley Spencer and Mona Mazur were going to be a match made in heaven.

"Do you think she's for real?" whispered Matilda, Ashley's mother, when Mona finally welcomed them, click-clacking across the sweeping expanse of black-and-white tiles to fetch one of her parties-of-the-rich-and-fabulous albums to show them what she could do.

Ashley nodded, entranced, twirling a strand of her long golden hair between two fingers. Mona was very glamorous in a fifties-pinup sort of way, her jet-black hair worn in a lacy snood, her pale skin almost translucent. She looked like a femme fatale in a black-and-white movie, the kind of dame who packed a pistol in her crocodile handbag.

"*You* should wear a snood," Ashley suggested, but Matilda just laughed. What was up with her mother this week? Like Mona, Matilda was pale, but not in a good way, like a powdered geisha, but more like she was washed out and drained of color.

Matilda had pulled her long blond hair into a stringy ponytail, and if it hadn't been for Ashley having a fit as they were climbing into their new bronze Porsche Cayenne, her mother would actually be sitting here right now still wearing socks and Birkenstocks.

Luckily, there was a pair of Tod's driving shoes under the front seat, because Matilda said she was too tired to go back in and change. Ashley's mother was one of those beautiful but not vain women who rarely shopped or dressed up. When pressed, Matilda could be counted on to wear something simple but elegant: beige linen in the summer, butter suede in the winter, and subtle jewelry all year round.

But she usually stuck to a wardrobe that had a ten-year-old expiration date: She was still wearing her J. Crew rugbys from college, and the Birkenstocks were taking it too far. Ashley was afraid Mona Mazur would take one look at the comfortable cork-soled shoes and shut the door in their faces.

"Now," said Mona, tapping back into the room and arranging the black-covered book on the coffee table in front of them. "May I offer you some tea, Mrs. Spencer?"

"That would be great." Matilda tugged at the neck of her cream sweater as though it was strangling her. "I'm not feeling . . . entirely a hundred percent right now."

"Chamomile, perhaps?" suggested Mona, waving two fingers in the air. Instantly, one of her doe-eyed assistants materialized to receive her orders.

Ashley flicked through the plastic pages of the book, eagerly skimming every picture of Moroccan-style bazaars, fake wintry forests, and re-creations of the *Titanic*'s ballroom. It was great to get ideas from other people's parties, but for her own, Ashley wanted something unique. Something bigger and better. After all, she was Ashley Spencer—the most envied twelve-year-old girl in San Francisco. This *had* to be the best Super-Sweet Thirteen party ever.

And she had other reasons for wanting this to be a party nobody in the Bay Area would ever forget. This semester wasn't going quite as smoothly as Ashley had hoped. At the beginning of the school year, everything was just perfect. The Ashleys were rocking Miss Gamble's. The Ashleys were the cutest, the best-dressed, the most feared girls in school, and Ashley was queen of the Ashleys. Everyone was so jealous when she snagged Tri Fitzpatrick, the cutest boy in the seventh grade at Gregory Hall, as her first real boyfriend.

But then things started going wrong. Tri never seemed to get around to kissing her, and he eventually told her he really preferred A.A.—Ashley Alioto, the tallest and sportiest of the Ashleys. Whatever!

Then she'd even let nouveau-riche Lauren Page into the Ashleys, since she could get them on the reality TV show *Preteen Queen*. But that was another thing that started out in Ashley's favor but suddenly turned sour. Just as she was ruling the airwaves and scoring all the votes, the network dumped the show. Losing a boyfriend and a reality show in one week would have broken the spirits of most girls her age, but Ashley had managed to make it look as if she hardly even noticed.

Even if she *was* currently the only one of the Ashleys to not have a boyfriend. Lili was dating Max, the cute guy from her French conversation class; A.A. was dating Hunter, the hot red-headed Gregory Hall goalie, and word had it that Lauren had not one but *two* boyfriends. Ashley shook her head and slammed the book shut, almost dislodging her mother's teacup. Everyone with a boyfriend but her: How did *that* happen?

Worst of all was the stupid blog, AshleyRank, that her father's lawyer had managed, at long last, to close down. Some sixth-grade wannabes had been making her life a misery, dropping her ranking from number one to a tragic number four. The most unforgivable offense: The blog had crowned a new queen—Ashley Li (better known as Lili) as the new ruler of the seventh grade.

Okay, so Lili was her best friend, and they were devoted to each other—but c'mon! Lili was a total copycat—always buying a pair of J Brand Love Story denims only after seeing Ashley's, always crushing on boys Ashley had declared adorable, always being the first to admire Ashley's new handbags.

Thank goodness AshleyRank was history, and Ashley

hoped that its demise had torpedoed the idea that *anyone* other than Ashley was numero uno as well. Her party would show them she was at the top of her game. All she needed was a little parental cooperation. And a huge party budget, of course.

Mona Mazur's parties cost more than most weddings.

"You know, sweetie," her mother said with a pained smile, rattling the saucer as she set down her teacup. "I wonder if we could come back another day to do this. I'm just not feeling very well right now."

"Mom!" Ashley whined. "Are you sure? Can you just hold it together for a little longer?" She looked at her mom worriedly. There was clearly something wrong with Matilda, but the thought of a sick parent was too scary to contemplate. Ashley hated whenever her parents fell ill, and she harbored nightmarish scenarios of being a poor, friendless orphan whenever they did.

Plus, her birthday was practically tomorrow, and nothing was planned yet. How would she know which outfits to buy if they hadn't decided on a theme? She squeezed her mother's arm and hoped it would communicate how important this was.

Luckily, Mona seemed to be on her side.

"Unfortunately, there's not much time to pull all this together, Mrs. Spencer," she said. "But we can make it quick, yes? Ashley, have you seen anything in my book that inspires you?"

7

"Well, yes and no," Ashley began, pausing when she glanced at her mother. Matilda really did look bad. Her forehead looked clammy, and she kept closing her eyes. Oh God. She would be a foster child. Or worse, sent to live with the Spencers' only living relative: batty Aunt Agnes, who lived in Vermont with two hundred sheep and made cheese.

Ashley started rattling off ideas as quickly as they formed in her head in order to shake the scary image of having to live among barn animals. "I was thinking of some kind of international theme. . . ."

"I was thinking of something more age-appropriate," her mother said faintly, as though she was too exhausted to continue, and she closed her eyes for a moment.

"Like the circus, perhaps?" Mona suggested, her face serene. "I think that would work very nicely with the space as well. You have those lovely cathedral ceilings, perfect for a tightrope. We could have rides and carnival attractions in the yard, fire-eaters on stilts along the entryway . . ."

"A circus?" Ashley was pouting. She didn't want anything too childish. It all sounded like a clowns-tying-balloons party, the kind of thing the Ashleys had always mocked.

"It can be very sophisticated," Mona explained. "Think of Cirque du Soleil."

"Yes." Ashley's mother stood up, shaky on her feet. "Let's

move ahead with that. Just send me the plan and the estimate. . . ."

"That's it?" Ashley blurted. So there was to be no more discussion? She crossed her arms and huffed. First her mother had to be *dragged* here, and now she was racing out the door before they'd even had a chance to discuss a circus-themed menu, how Ashley was going to make a grand entrance on a Vespa, or how many lions they could fit in the den. Everything was being left to chance. Well, chance and Mona. But planning was half the fun!

"I'm sorry." Her mother offered a limp hand to Mona. "I just don't feel very . . . BLEAAGH!"

And with that, Matilda Spencer vomited all over the coffee table, her teacup, and Mona's famous black book, all over her shoes, and all over the snow-white sheepskin rug.

The place was covered in lime green vomit.

"Omigod!" shrieked Ashley, jumping to her feet. "Mom! Are you okay?" She looked at her mother, stricken with fear and disgust. Nimble Mona had leaped from her stool and avoided getting splattered, but Dorothy the poodle wasn't so lucky: She'd been prancing past just as her mother started barfing and was now dripping with what looked like a mess of regurgitated peas.

Ashley put a hand on her mother's elbow, shocked speechless. She hoped it was just food poisoning and not

9

something more serious. Nothing that would mean Ashley would live out the rest of her life having to wear itchy wool sweaters and eat Aunt Agnes's horrible cooking. Matilda was bent double, one trembling hand holding back her ponytail. Mona looked concerned and just a tiny bit appalled.

Uh-oh. Maybe this was going to be a deal breaker. Maybe Mona didn't like clients who threw up their lunches all over the black-and-white decor, even if those lunches were organic and prepared by a private chef. Maybe she'd show them the door and badmouth them to all the other party planners in San Francisco.

But even as she was anxious about her mother's health, Ashley couldn't help but wonder: What did this mean for her Super-Sweet Thirteen?

2

WHY'D HE HAVE TO GO AND MAKE THINGS SO "COMPLICATED"? ACTING LIKE SOMEBODY ELSE IS MAKING LILI FRUSTRATED

THIS WAS NOT LILI'S KIND OF PLACE: CHEAP, gritty, and so *unhygienic* it was practically a health hazard. She cradled her chunky off-white coffee cup to avoid taking another sip of the generic-diner coffeelike liquid that was now lukewarm and completely bitter, nothing at all like her favorite café mochas.

Sure the diner was near Fillmore, major stomping ground for the Ashleys—they met at the Fillmore Starbucks every morning before school—but this divey roach trap was *off* Fillmore, "off" being the operative word. None of the other Ashleys would dream of coming in here, Lili was sure of that.

Oh well. At least none of her friends would spot her. The things she was doing for love!

Hanging out at the diner was Max's idea. As in Max Costa, her boyfriend. He'd only been her boyfriend for two minutes, since their dramatic reunion at the *Preteen Queen* results party, but Lili was learning fast that relationships with boys weren't quite as . . . well, romantic as she'd expected.

Especially when your boyfriend went to Arthur Reed Prep School for the Arts, where everyone spent all their time pretending to be artsy and unconventional. So there they were, squeezed into a sticky vinyl booth with his best buds, Jason Brooks and Quentin Del Rosario, talking about what they always talked about with Max's friends—their emo band's MySpace page.

Lili's mind drifted away from the conversation, and she lowered her coffee cup, shaking her dark curls. Sure, Max was hunky and blond, but it was easier to cast him in the role of McDreamy when he was smoldering across the room at a party. Not so easy when he and his friends were competing to see who could come up with the most obscure references to garage bands and underground movies.

She tried to suppress a sigh, thinking about Ashley and how this was the day Ashley and her mom were meeting the party planner extraordinaire, Mona Mazur. Now *that* was a Saturday-afternoon activity Lili could get excited about.

Party planning was her thing—hadn't she organized the best mixer ever at Miss Gamble's earlier this semester? Of course, her best friend had almost died at the event, but that wasn't her fault. Besides, Ashley had more than bounced back from beyond the grave.

Unfortunately, things were kind of chilly between the two of them at the moment. Even if AshleyRank had been shut down, Lili knew that Ashley would never forgive her for nabbing the top spot. Although once again, Lili had nothing to do with it. The people had spoken!

For a heady moment, Lili had toyed with the fantasy of kicking Ashley out of the Ashleys and making Ashley's humiliation complete. But Ashley proved a lot more resilient than her svelte frame suggested, and she had recouped social losses by talking up her blowout birthday bash to anyone and everyone. Still, Lili liked knowing that Ashley's prominence would never be taken for granted again—least of all by Lili.

Now that she had Max around, it was harder to make time out of school for the Ashleys anyway.

"Could you move over?" asked a snooty voice, and Lili's heart sank. Jason and Quentin had brought their girlfriends with them—Cassandra Allison (Lili thought it was odd to have two names that were first names, but whatever) and Jezebel Jackson-Green, both seventh-graders at Reed too—and the girls were back from a ten-minute bathroom trip.

Both wore torn skinny black jeans, white wife beaters, and too much black eyeliner. Cassandra had on an over-size khaki fatigue jacket, and her dyed-red, greasy bangs looked like they'd been dipped in raspberry sauce. Jezebel (whose real name was Jennifer, Lili found out later) had a pierced nostril, and her mousy hair tied up with an oil-stained bandanna. They made Lili want to wrinkle her pert little nose.

She wriggled over in the booth, scrunching up next to Max to make room for Cassandra, while Jezebel plopped down on the other side of the table, next to Jason. Lili just knew that the two girls had been bitching about her in the bathroom. Though why they were acting so superior was beyond her. Hello—was there a mirror in the bathroom? Had they *seen* how stupid they looked? Grunge was so over. Even Avril was now toting Vuitton bags.

"So, Lili," said Cassandra, glancing over at Jezebel's smirking face. "How do you feel about camping? Max is really into it, you know."

"Um . . ." Lili was flustered for a moment. She didn't know that Max was into camping. She barely knew *anything* about him, apart from the fact that he was a star player on the lacrosse team (a fluke, apparently, at boho heaven Reed Prep), that he spoke fluent French (and only took French conversation to sharpen his skills), and that he rode a skateboard and played in a band. He was cute and he liked her. What else was there to know? She inadvertently nudged him with her leg, but he didn't even notice. The guys were still engrossed in band talk. "I guess so. I mean, why not?"

"Really?" Jezebel screwed up her face. "You don't look like the outdoor type."

"Neither do you," Lili retorted. It came out sharper and ruder than she intended, but really! Both of the girls were as pale as ghosts. Apart from the red smudges of oversqueezed zits, that is.

"My parents take us hiking in the Sierra Nevadas every summer," said Jezebel, a strange glint in her unusually milky blue eyes. "My dad is, like, a *woodsman.*" Uh-huh. Jezebel's dad ran a hedge fund.

"Yeah, and our families let us go camping up on Mount Tam all the time." Cassandra ran her pale, ink-stained fingers through her dyed bangs. "They believe in kids being independent, learning to fend for themselves. Have you ever been camping?"

"Probably . . ." Lili tried to play for time. "I don't really remember, exactly."

"Either you have or you haven't." Jezebel rolled her eyes.

"God, you've totally missed out!" said Cassandra, elbowing Lili. Just what Lili needed—scaly flakes of skin from Cassandra's dry, moisturizer-deprived arms on her new black suede Daryl K jacket! "Are your parents really over-protective or something?"

"Or maybe they think you're just *too young*?" Jezebel asked with a curled lip, and the look she and Cassandra exchanged suggested that this was exactly what they thought. They were acting as though she was a complete baby.

"Of course not," Lili said quickly. Her heart was beating fast. "They let me do whatever I want." Which was not at all true. Her parents were pretty strict.

"Even go camping on Mount Tam?" Cassandra sounded skeptical.

"'Course!" Lili lied, looking down at the dregs of her coffee cup. "Mount Tam" was Mount Tamalpais, just north of the Golden Gate, but it might as well have been north of the Arctic Circle as far as Lili was concerned. Her family was definitely not the camping type. More like the five-star-hotel type.

Her father, Charles Li, was a Silicon Valley CEO, and his idea of relaxing was flying up to Napa for a weekend in his prop plane to buy cases of wine for his cellar. Her mother, Nancy Khan, was an ex-high-powered lawyer who now chan-neled her excess energies into Miss Gamble's board of trustees meetings and haranguing her daughters' private tutors. Their house in Presidio Heights was as big as a small nation, so there was always a battalion of staff members for her mother to manage—including two nannies, one each for Lili's adorable little sisters, Josephine and Brennan, and two personal assistants for her mother's charity and social events.

Lili had more extracurricular activities and classes to attend than the entire seventh grade of Miss Gamble's combined, from music and language lessons to assisting a genetic researcher at Stanford. Whenever her two older sisters were back from college or boarding school for any length of time, the whole family flew to Taiwan to visit relatives. Her mother's idea of roughing it was to fly first class rather than charter a jet. When—and why—would they ever go camping?

Not that Lili would ever suggest such a thing to her parents in the first place. The shoes people wore when they went camping were just plain ugly. Who wanted to wear giant work boots or those sandals with congealed-black-rubber soles and straps made out of Velcro? Not any of the Ashleys, that was certain. She couldn't help shuddering at the thought.

"Are you cold?" Max asked. "I could ask them to turn up the thermostat."

Lili shook her head and returned his smile. At least he was paying her some attention at last. He reached across the table and squeezed her hand. With his fine blond hair and inky-dark eyes, he was so striking. She could almost forgive him for dragging her to a place like this and abandoning her to these witchy alterna-wannabes.

"We were just talking about the camping trip to Mount Tam," said Cassandra, leaning across Lili like she wasn't there. Lili flinched: Cassandra's hair smelled gummy and looked like it hadn't been washed in three days. At least she didn't have to worry about Max dumping her for some girl at his own school—they made the Helena Academy pigs look like debutantes.

"Yeah, I meant to mention it." Max sounded sheepish. "We've been talking about it at school."

"Lili wants to go," chimed in Jezebel from across the table. "Don't you, Lili?"

Lili nodded and tried her best to smile. Not only did she *not* want to go, she would never be allowed to go. Not in a million years. Her parents would think it was absurdly dangerous, especially at this time of the year. And they would never agree to a coed camping trip, whatever the season.

Her parents didn't even know Max was her boyfriend—for one very good reason: Lili wasn't allowed to have a boyfriend. *Any* boyfriend. Not until she was fifteen, two long years away. Nobody knew about this rule, not even the other Ashleys. This afternoon she'd told her mother she was meeting A.A. at the Fillmore Starbucks to plan a science project and then ducked around the corner once Nancy's black hybrid SUV was out of sight.

"It would be so cool if you could come." Max's smile was

bright: It lit up his whole face. "I wasn't sure if you'd be able to."

"Yeah." Cassandra sighed, giving a mock-sympathetic shrug. "You probably won't be allowed, right?"

"Hey, Max—it's okay," Jezebel said. "We can invite another girl from school to make up the numbers."

"My sister could come," Quentin suggested, snapping his checkerboard suspenders.

"I'll go!" Lili almost shouted. No way was she going to be jostled aside by Courtney Love's godchildren. No way were they going to get away with implying she was an over-privileged, overprotected princess who was too delicate to go on a camping trip. Lili was good at everything she set her mind to—why should camping be any different?

"That's great." Max beamed. "We were thinking about two weekends from now, before it starts getting really cold. Will that be okay?"

"Sure." Lili nodded, but her heart was pounding. With her overscheduled life, it was hard enough lying to her mother about a few hours in the city. How was she going to get away with a whole weekend up on Mount Tam?

3

A.A. WALKS THE THIN LINE
BETWEEN LOVE AND HATE

A.A. DRUMMED HER FINGERS IMPATIENTLY on the cracked wooden table, trying to focus on the vintage black-and-white photos lining the opposite wall. This was Buzz Burgers, one of her favorite places to eat, especially when she wasn't with the other Ashleys. Unlike her best friends, A.A. actually liked to eat, especially on a Saturday evening in November after she'd played a boisterous game of soccer in the afternoon. She loved how the fresh, brisk, soon-to-be winter wind felt on her skin.

She didn't even mind eating in public, unlike Ashley Spencer, who would rather starve than be seen in public consuming anything larger than an olive—even if it meant scarfing a pint of ice cream when she got home. And Lili never let food pass her lips if (a) there were boys around,

(b) the restaurant wasn't scrupulously immaculate and scrubbed clean, or (c) Ashley Spencer wasn't eating. Those two would faint from hunger before conceding in front of each other. It was a totally ridiculous competition, and A.A. was always glad she wasn't part of it.

Tall and slim, with a super-speedy metabolism, sports-mad A.A. could get away with eating like a boy. Her fashion-model mother kept warning her that she couldn't keep stuffing her face forever, but A.A. was going to enjoy every minute of eating like a whale while she could. And there was nothing in the world she liked to eat as much as a huge, juicy burger, dripping with melted cheese and crammed into a lightly toasted bun—just the way Buzz made them.

But tonight she couldn't wait to get out of this place. Sure, she was looking forward to the food arriving. A.A. kept telling herself that by the time she'd silently counted all the photos on the wall her burger would arrive and the worst part of the evening would be over. Because then she could eat, and once she had eaten, she could get out of here.

"Hey, do you want to try some of this soup?" Hunter's voice broke her concentration. Ugh! Now she'd lost count.

"It's okay," she said, giving him a quick grin. He probably thought she was acting weird, and that was too bad—it wasn't his fault. Hunter was her boyfriend, and he was a nice guy, even if he did have hair that looked like a bunch of uprooted carrots. Hunter knew she liked this place, which was why he'd suggested it. He was that kind of guy—thoughtful, in a low-key kind of way. They'd only been dating for a month, and he tried to hang out with her as much as their schedules allowed. He'd even come to watch her play soccer that afternoon once his crew practice was over (lacrosse season had ended).

Hunter, sitting on her right and scooping up another giant mouthful of clam chowder, wasn't the problem. The problem was on the other side of the table. Specifically, Tri Fitzpatrick—the boy who used to date Ashley Spencer.

The boy who used to be A.A.'s best friend, the guy who lived in a luxurious private apartment in the Fairmont Hotel, just like she did. The boy she'd kissed at a Seven Minutes in Heaven party, the boy who acted like he was totally into her. A.A. still didn't understand what had happened between her and Tri—one day they were best friends, then suddenly it was as if they hardly knew each other at all. One day they were kissing, the next day he acted like it had never happened. A.A. just didn't get him.

And there was something else she didn't get. It had been only a couple of weeks since Ashley had broken up with him after the *Preteen Queen* party, and Tri had already found another girlfriend. Her name was Cecily, and he'd brought her along tonight. A double date—Tri's idea. Cecily was sitting there next to him in Buzz Burgers, holding his hand. At least Hunter had the sense to eat his soup and not paw at her like a lovesick puppy every few minutes.

That's what she liked about Hunter—he didn't push. They didn't have to make out every second to show the world they liked each other. Of course, they kissed—what couple didn't? But it was nothing like the kiss she'd experienced with Tri. Not that she was comparing. Kissing Hunter felt comfortable and safe. It didn't have the same dizzying energy as kissing Tri, but maybe that was for the best. Maybe Tri's kiss had been memorable merely because it was the only one they would ever share.

Forty-four, forty-five, forty-six . . . the waitress took away Hunter's scraped-clean bread bowl. . . . Forty-seven, forty-eight, forty-nine . . . was that their food? No, it was another table's. . . . Fifty, fifty-one, fifty-two . . . God, what was Tri's disagreeable girlfriend jabbering about now?

"I wish I hadn't ordered a burger," Cecily lamented, rubbing her flat-as-a-washboard stomach with the hand that Tri wasn't clinging to. Great—just what the world needed. Another girl talking about her teensy-weensy appetite, pretending to boys that she lived on a handful of almonds and a teaspoon of low-fat salad dressing. Cecily gestured with her head (she had the Posh Spice bob) to the next table. "They just look *huge*."

"That's the point," A.A. said, knowing she sounded snippy, but she didn't care. They were at Buzz Burgers, get it? If she wanted to hang out with picky eaters, she'd rather be with Ashley and Lili anytime.

"Not everyone knows that." Suddenly Tri was talking to her, after not directing a single word to her all evening. "But then I guess you know everything."

A.A.'s mouth fell open. Whenever they saw each other these days, it felt like Tri was angry at *her*. What was up with that? He was the one who'd kissed her in the closet while he was still officially going out with Ashley. He was the one who said he was planning to break up with Ashley, and then—the *very next day*—went round to Ashley's house to beg her forgiveness and tell her she was the only girl in the world. And now that Ashley had dumped him, he'd instantly pounced on a new girlfriend. He was a grade-A jerk.

"Here's our food," Hunter said, sounding relieved, as the waitress swooped down on them with dinner plates as large as trays. At least he wouldn't force A.A. into another hideous double date. She stopped trying to think of a nasty response to Tri's rude comment and focused on the burger in front of her—a towering mass of meaty deliciousness in the middle of a sea of golden, crinkled fries.

"So, what's it like at Miss Gamble's?" Cecily was trying to make polite conversation, carefully squeezing a pool of ketchup onto the side of her plate.

"It's cool." A.A. shrugged, her mouth full. Cecily didn't

even go to school: She and her sisters had private tutors, since they had to travel so often. Her parents owned swanky hotels and resorts around the globe, including one recently renovated hotel in San Francisco. That was how Tri had met her, at some hoteliers association get-together his parents had dragged him to. It was a dynastic match, A.A. thought, taking another huge bite out of her burger. Next Tri would be going out with Paris Hilton!

"I hear you guys get to do lots of fun things there." Cecily nibbled on a fry and gave A.A. a nervous smile. A.A. stared hard at her, trying to decide if she was being sarcastic or malicious in any way, but Cecily looked sincere. "Like the big party where you turned your school gym into a nightclub? It sounded so cool."

"It's not really a gym," A.A. told her. Miss Gamble's wouldn't have anything as tacky as a *gym*, but it wasn't Cecily's fault she didn't know that. All the girl knew about junior high was from TV and movies.

"I wish my parents would let me go there." Cecily sighed. "It'd be so cool to meet other kids my age and have tons of friends."

A.A. chewed a particularly juicy mouthful, feeling kind of bad for Cecily. She clearly had no idea that making friends at school was *way* more complicated than just showing up. She should ask Lauren Page. Lauren was rejected—make that *shunned*—for years until her father's website, YourTV.com, went through the roof and she walked into school with new clothes, new hair, and a new body. And even then the Ashleys snubbed her until she could deliver something they really wanted, like spots in the *Preteen Queen* reality show.

She liked Lauren, even though it seemed like sometimes Lauren was trying too hard to get them to like her and should just chill out. Cecily obviously thought girls' schools were cozy and sweet. She wouldn't last five minutes at Miss Gamble's.

Tri snorted. "Ces, that place is like a shark pit. They'd eat you alive."

A.A. glared at him. It was one thing for *her* to think that, but quite another for Tri Fitzpatrick to be badmouthing her school all over the Bay Area.

"That's because some Gregory Hall boys are too immature for Miss Gamble's girls," she explained to Cecily, ripping her slice of pickle in two and wishing it was Tri's arm. "You know how it is. Some guys just can't handle strong women. They're too scared."

"You'd be scared as well." Tri was talking to Cecily but shooting A.A. the evil eye. "You should really steer clear of that place."

"If you don't want those fries, I'll have them." Hunter gestured at A.A.'s plate, his hand creeping over. He was totally oblivious to the conversation, his eyes focused on the game playing on a flat-screen television above the counter.

"You can have some of mine," offered Cecily. "Usually I'd eat all of this, but my grandparents took me and my sisters out to Ruth's Chris for lunch and I really stuffed my face. Sorry to be such a killjoy. I hate it when girls pretend they don't eat."

A.A. wasn't sure what was worse—Cecily being a dainty little namby-pamby, or Cecily being not that bad. Almost normal, in fact. If circumstances were different, A.A. might even like her.

"Last time Ces and I went out for dinner, we ordered these giant sundaes and had an eating contest," Tri bragged. If he was talking to Hunter, he was wasting his time—Hunter was preoccupied shoveling forkloads of Cecily's fries onto his own plate. "And she totally won!"

"Tri's used to losing at things," A.A. couldn't resist saying, gazing over at Cecily's innocent face rather than look at Tri's annoying one. "I've kicked his ass from here to Toronto in every video game known to man."

"As if that's something to be proud of," scoffed Tri. "Macho is real attractive on a chick. See what I was talking about, Ces? You should go home tonight and thank your parents for keeping you away from Miss Gamble's."

"Actually, I think that's pretty cool she's so good at games," Cecily began, her face flushing.

27

A chick? Since when did Tri call her a "chick"? A.A. was furious. "You're embarrassing yourself," she told Tri. "Why don't you pick on someone *your own size*?"

Now it was Tri's turn to go red. He was pretty sensitive these days about being the shortest seventh grader at Gregory Hall.

"I can't believe you guys are letting all this great food go to waste," said Hunter, greedily eying A.A.'s plate again. "I thought you were hungry."

"I've lost my appetite." A.A. pushed her plate away.

"Alert the media," mumbled Tri, sullenly picking up the soggy remains of a bun and pushing it into his mouth. A.A. was furious with him. How dare he be so rude to her in front of Cecily? And in front of her own boyfriend? Tri should know better than to mess with someone twice his height and triple his intelligence. If this was the way he wanted to play it, then okay.

Tri wanted war? A.A. would give him war.

4

LAUREN FINDS DOUBLE-DEALING JUST LEADS TO DOUBLE TROUBLE

THE SLEEK BENTLEY CONTINENTAL PURRED up to the main gates of Miss Gamble's and slid into one of the spaces reserved for dropping off and picking up pupils—all of the spaces empty now, because it was eleven on a Monday morning and school had been in session for a couple of hours. Lauren Page, in the Bentley's backseat, leaned forward for a last-minute check of her hair and lip gloss in the console mirror.

She'd just been to the dentist, and she had to make sure there was no trace of anything powdery or sticky around her mouth. Last year she wouldn't have thought twice about this: She'd have been rubbing her sore jaw, or obsessing over being late for class. But that was then, and this was now.

Once upon a time, Lauren had dreaded Monday mornings. She used to dread walking up to the main gates of Miss Gamble's, because that meant walking past the Ashleys. Every morning they'd be posed on a stone bench by the playground like vengeful Greek goddesses, scrutinizing every girl as she arrived, making snide comments about the way they wore their school uniform or their hair.

Before this semester, Lauren came to school on the bus, not in a Bentley. Her heart would thud as she got off one stop early—so none of the other girls would see her taking public transportation. When she approached the school, she would put her head down and scurry by as quickly as she could, wishing she were invisible.

And usually she *was* invisible to the Ashleys; they were far more concerned with wannabes and potential style rivals than hopeless cases. Because that was exactly what Lauren used to be—a hopeless case. Frizzy hair, bad skin, thick glasses, baby fat, no makeup, secondhand clothes. Someone no one paid attention to, whose name was only mentioned at school prize-giving, when she snagged all the awards.

Then, last summer, Lauren's computer-nerd father hit the Silicon Valley gold mine. She got tanned, toned, and terrific, and everything changed. She made it her goal to join the most exclusive clique in school: the Ashleys. There'd been some speed bumps along the way—winning over the trio of baby barracudas wasn't easy. But for now, she was IN. She was one of them.

It was all part of her secret master plan: to bring the Ashleys down. To destroy them once and for all. Lauren had weathered years of ridicule and misery at their snotty hands. In kindergarten, Ashley Spencer had said in front of the whole class, "Everyone is invited to my birthday party except for Lauren Page!" while in fourth grade, Lili had made up the nickname "Loron" (a clever combo of "Lauren" and "moron," and a name that stuck for years) just to amuse Ashley, and last year, A.A. had picked her last once again for a volleyball tournament during PE. Lauren vowed she would have her revenge one day.

Becoming an Ashley was just the first step. Because as every good spy knows, corruption always starts from within.

Luckily, that silly blog, AshleyRank, had started her work for her. The key to power, as Lauren was learning this semester in honors history, was divide and conquer. When the now-defunct blog started toying with the Ashleys, shooting Lauren into the upper echelons and demoting Queen Bee Ashley Spencer to number four, fault lines had appeared in the heretofore solid coalition of cool.

Okay, so maybe up-close and personal, the Ashleys weren't as evil as Lauren had originally believed them to be. They were almost sweet. A.A. gave big, friendly smiles and made her feel like one of the gang. Lili had included her in the dance squad at the Gregory Hall lacrosse game. Ashley had even helped her shop for clothes before the big "Seven" party. They weren't *all* bad. And now that she was an Ashley herself, did she really want to give all this up?

"Here we are—better late than never," Dex said, grinning at Lauren in the rearview mirror. "Are you gonna sit there all day gazing at yourself? Some of us have things to do."

"What, like drop off the dry cleaning?" Lauren retorted. Dex was like a big brother to her, as well as her driver. He was her father's intern—or protégé, as Dex preferred to call it. He wasn't even eighteen yet, but he seemed to enjoy giving Lauren endless advice about her life. And she enjoyed telling him to mind his own business.

"Better than dropping a filling into my food." Dex scratched his buzz cut, probably to drown out the sound of Lauren's theatrical sigh. He just couldn't stop bringing that up, could he? Ever since one of Lauren's fillings had clunked onto her plate at Sunday brunch, to her mother's horror and Dex's delight, he'd worked it into every possible conversation.

Worst of all, he said—right there at the table, in front of her parents—that fillings often came loose when you spent too much time kissing. How embarrassing! Her father just held up the newspaper and pretended not to hear, while (even more excruciating) her mother looked all overjoyed, leaning over to stroke Lauren's hair and talk about how popular her baby was these days. *Eek!*

It was bad enough trying to juggle two boyfriends without discussing the gory details with your parents! And all the deception was exhausting. Pretending to be a friend to the Ashleys while secretly plotting their demise and pretending to be the only girlfriend of two guys took a whole lot of energy.

Dating two guys *sounded* like fun until you actually had to do it. Just keeping them straight—and keeping them apart— was practically a full-time job. Lauren had a good memory, and she knew it was dark-haired Alex who'd lived in Spain for a summer and wanted to grow up to be a famous film director, while towhead Christian was the one whose parents were divorced and whose biggest ambition was to ski every top mountain in the world.

But the other day she'd absentmindedly mentioned to Alex how her language arts teacher with the bad breath reminded her of the fire-breathing beast in the latest monster movie, which got him confused, and she'd had to say "never mind" when she realized too late that it was Christian with whom she'd seen the latest smash-up-New-York blockbuster.

Her phone rang with a thumping hip-hop beat: boyfriend number one, Christian (favorite band: Flo Rida). If it had rung with the sound of an orchestral symphony with a punk-pop edge, that would mean it was boyfriend number two: Alex (favorite band: Vampire Weekend).

"Hey there!" She smiled into her phone, ignoring Dex's ear-to-ear smirk from the front seat. "How was your presentation?" She had helped Christian come up with an argument for his public speaking class's debate—Spiderman: Superhero or Super Fool?

She laughed when he made a joke about his spidey sense tingling. "Me? I'm just about to walk into school. Just got back from the mental dental. Ugh. Two cavities. I know. This afternoon? Sure, I'd love to—oh." She just remembered. She'd promised Alex they would study for their Latin midterms after school together. "Oh, you know what, I can't. I've got late study hall. Yeah, it sucks. Okay, maybe tomorrow. Cool."

Lauren caught Dex's eye in the mirror as she hung up. She knew he knew she didn't have late study hall, which was Miss Gamble's—speak for detention. "Don't start," she warned him.

She felt like a total snake for lying to Christian, and she hated herself for it. It was torture, feeling like she was cheating all the time. The problem was that she liked both of them so much. Alex was incredibly handsome, while Christian was the only boy who could make her laugh so hard Diet Coke came snorting out of her nose. She knew she had to decide whom she liked better at some point, but the thought of hurting their feelings made her stomach feel so twisted up that she convinced herself dating the two of them at the same time was a much nicer thing to do than dumping one of them.

"Do you think I'm a bad person?" Lauren asked, hoping to get a straight answer for a change.

Dex merely chuckled. "Feeling guilty, Little Miss Man-Eater?"

She shrugged, wishing Dex would take her seriously, but whenever she tried to have a heart-to-heart, it was obvious he thought her situation was hilarious. He was no help at all. Worse, he began to sing some cheesy old song called "Torn Between Two Lovers."

"Okay. Enough!" She opened the car door and slithered out. She was wearing a curvy Balenciaga crested blazer over her uniform—the newest Ashley fashion statement. "Try not to overdo it today," she told him, full of mock concern, pausing before she closed the door. "I know how hard it is for you to think of more than one thing at a time."

"Remember what the dentist said," Dex called after her as she walked through the gates. "Not too much oral action for a few days!"

Lauren ignored this, as well as the obnoxious kissing sounds he was making, and marched up the stone stairs with as much dignity as she could muster. If she hurried, she'd only miss the first five minutes of honors history.

5

ASHLEY TELLS HERSELF IT'S NOT A LIE IF YOU BELIEVE IT'S THE TRUTH

C AN YOU BELIEVE HE HAS A NEW GIRL-
friend already?"

"Huh?" Ashley looked up from her Chanel compact. She wasn't paying attention to what A.A. was saying. She wanted to check if the tiny red dot she'd discovered on her nose that morning was still there. Yep. It sure was. She pressed some more powder on the affected area.

It was all her mother's fault. Matilda spent all her time lazing about on the couch napping and couldn't be bothered to take care of any party details. The stress from having birthdaypalooza turn into birthdaypa*bust* was making her break out. Ashley frowned at the cakey bump. Isn't that why they called it concealer? Because it concealed things? But every time she patted on another layer, it was like she was drawing a huge arrow pointing to the middle of her face, flashing: ZIT! ZIT! ZIT!

"Are you even listening to me?" A.A. snapped. The two of them were exiting the regular history classroom and walking toward the hallway where Lili and Lauren were going to meet them after their honors history class. The four of them would then proceed to the refectory together. The Ashleys liked to make an entrance, and walking into a room, four in a row, always had the desired effect.

Ashley gave her friend a sweet smile and put away her makeup. She would just have to live with being less than perfect for the time being. At least until she got a mini-facial at Bliss. "Of course. You were talking about Hunter, right? He's so gorge."

"Um, no. I was talking about Tri."

"Tri?" Ashley scrunched her nose as if she'd smelled something bad.

A.A. sighed. "Your ex-boyfriend?"

"Right." Ashley wondered why on earth A.A. thought she would be interested in Tri's love life, since he was no longer part of hers.

A.A. bit a cuticle off her thumb. "He's dating someone new. I met her the other night."

"So?"

"So you don't care?"

"Why should I care, he dum—I mean, I dumped him. Once you take out the trash, it doesn't matter who picks it up from the curb." Ashley sighed. She glared at a sixth grader who was impudently staring at her—and not with the usual fear and worship. Maybe it was because of her humongous zit? Ugh! Great, now everyone would think she was a leper.

A.A. absentmindedly swung her slouchy new Yves Saint Laurent Downtown bag (the new Ashley school-bag of choice) back and forth, almost slamming the large patent-leather accessory into Ashley. "I know. But you don't feel weirded out that he would move on so quickly?"

"Not really," Ashley said airily. She wished they would get off the subject. She still felt a little guilty whenever A.A. talked about Tri. The thing was, just a few weeks ago she'd told A.A. a little white lie—that *she* had dumped Tri, when the truth was the other way around. Tri had chucked her over the side because he'd kissed A.A. at a Seven Minutes in Heaven party and realized he was in love with A.A. all along. Okay, so maybe it wasn't very nice of her to lie to one of her BFFs, but what Tri had done to her wasn't so nice either.

Besides, Ashley was just about to dump *him*, really, as she was tired of waiting for him to kiss her, and hearing that he'd kissed A.A. was just the last straw. Tri got a jump on the dumping before she could, so it was simply a technicality about who dumped whom. Which made what she'd told

A.A. not really a lie. At least, not one that truly counted.

It wasn't as if A.A. liked Tri or anything like that. A.A. was always saying how short he was and how irritatingly conceited he was and how they never even hung out anymore. Besides, A.A. had that hot boyfriend, Hunter, so what was her problem?

"Hey, pretties," Lili broke in, carrying the Uptown version of the Yves Saint Laurent bag, which had a structured frame and polished hardware but was just as large. Honors history always let out a few minutes after regular because of all the homework their teacher gave out.

"Hey yourself," Ashley responded somewhat grumpily, as she didn't feel very pretty that day, what with the huge crater on her face. It didn't help that Lili looked fabulous—clear, dewy skin, sparkling eyes, glossy hair—making Ashley feel even more wretched. Maybe AshleyRank was right. Maybe Ashley was yesterday's news. She should just go move to Vermont with Aunt Agnes and hoover up cheese for the rest of her life.

"Guys, what am I going to do about this camping trip?" Lili asked, looking worried. "I have to go, I can't let those wenches win. I'm getting nightmares that they'll bring some other dreadhead slut who'll steal Max away."

Ashley felt better after hearing about Lili's Outward Bound worries. At least she just had a pimple to worry about, not a pair of pampered poseurs. "We'll think of something."

"We always do," A.A. agreed.

"Where's Lauren?" asked Ashley, noticing that the newest member of their group wasn't following behind Lili like she always was.

"Dunno," Lili said. "She was right behind me."

Ashley looked down the hall and spotted Lauren hanging by the doorway, talking to someone she couldn't see.

"Lauren? Coming?" she called.

Instead of running over with a syrupy compliment like she always did, Lauren hesitated, turning to the person she was speaking to and then looking back to Ashley with a somewhat tense smile on her face. "Go ahead, I'll catch up with you guys in a bit," she told them.

"Let's go, I'm starved," Lili urged.

Ashley shrugged. A.A. nodded, and the three of them walked to the refectory. The Ashleys waited for no one.

6

LAUREN TRIES TO DODGE
A BLAST FROM THE PAST

CHRISTIAN HAD TEXTED HER ALL THROUGH-
out class, and Lauren spent the hour furiously
replying to him, her fingers flying on the
phone hidden underneath her desk. Cell phones were
supposedly banned on school grounds, but that didn't
stop anyone from using them. The girls of Miss Gamble's
could send a text with their eyes closed.

She was so engrossed in their text flirtation that she
didn't pay attention to anything in class and didn't even notice
that the lunch bell had rung and that people were getting up
from their seats. She tapped a hasty good-bye to Christian and
gathered her books into her new YSL bag (which still gave her
a bit of sticker shock, but as they say, when an Ashley, spend as
an Ashley) when she felt a tap on her arm.

Standing in front of her was a new girl who seemed to know her name and looked way too familiar.

"Lauren—is that you?" The girl was tall and skinny in a gawky, all-elbows way, her school uniform hanging like a sack. Her lank fair hair was pulled into two childish braids, and she wore the kind of thick reading glasses that the Ashleys always referred to as plane windows. "It's Sadie—Sadie Graham!"

"Omigod!" Lauren almost dropped her phone. She totally remembered her now. Sadie had left Miss Gamble's in the middle of fourth grade when her parents moved to Connecticut. When Sadie left, Lauren had had nobody, really, except the other social rejects, and they weren't really her friends, just comrades in despair.

But Sadie was different. She was the only girl at school Lauren ever really liked. They used to sit together in the back row of every class and study together after school, rolling their eyes about the Ashleys. Sadie always insisted that the Ashleys were a bunch of stuck-up losers who were jealous of their superior brainpower, and of course Lauren always agreed.

"I tried to get your attention in class, but you never looked up from your desk. Anyway, my dad's company moved him back here. Can you believe it?" Sadie asked, beaming with happiness, pushing her thick black plastic glasses up onto the bridge of her nose. "I'm so happy you're still here!"

"Uh . . . yeah, that's . . . that's great." Lauren felt as

though time had frozen. As though *she* was frozen. She was still holding her notebook and pen over her open bag, unable to move from the spot. She felt a rush of conflicting emotions—she was truly happy and surprised to see Sadie again, but she was also completely taken aback.

Sadie knew Lauren when she had an unfortunate Shakira perm and wore patchy, cast-off sweaters rather than brand-new cashmere. When she was a social pariah. When the Ashleys didn't even know she existed.

Lauren looked anxiously to see if Lili, the only Ashley in honors history, had noticed Sadie talking to her. Lauren would totally lose major cool points if she were seen talking to a total zero like Sadie. While Lauren hated herself a little bit for thinking like that, it was the brutal truth. If she wasn't careful, one tiny slip and she would lose her precarious position at the top of the social pyramid.

The Ashleys would *never* speak to someone who looked and talked and acted like Sadie. Sadie was like Lauren last semester—a nobody.

Lauren noticed that Lili was waiting impatiently by the door, and she felt her stomach sink when she saw that Ashley and A.A. were now out in the hallway waiting too. Ashley even craned her neck and called for her.

She had to get rid of them without letting them see whom she was with. Quickly.

Lauren yelled back an excuse, hoping they would leave. One thing she could always count on was how self-centered the Ashleys were. They wouldn't hang out forever. Sure enough, they soon disappeared down the hallway. Lauren couldn't help but feel a little bad at being left behind so easily.

"You look so cute! I barely recognized you," said Sadie, frowning as though Lauren's cuteness might be a bad thing.

"You look . . . um . . . just the same!" Lauren was telling the truth. Sadie might be taller now, with bigger (and thicker) glasses, but she hadn't really changed. She still looked beaky and awkward. Lauren was the one who'd changed.

"I can't wait to hear all the gossip. Does Sheridan Riley still get those coughing fits? Does Guinevere Parker still eat erasers? And what about those mean girls—what were they called? The Ashleys? Are they still around?"

"Um," Lauren stalled.

"Anyway, wanna have lunch? I'm so hungry. I remember how wonderful the food is here." Sadie was smiling, as though coming back to Miss Gamble's and finding her old friend again was the best thing that had ever happened to her. "The food at Greenwich was awful. Some kind of stew every day. Does Cass Franklin still sit in quarantine?"

"No, and um, they changed the menu so the food's not so great here anymore." Lauren felt icy cold, and then flushed and hot. Sadie clearly expected them to eat lunch together. They used to every day, once upon a time, when Lauren was still a frog and not a princess. How could Lauren explain to her that everything had changed? That now she not only looked like an Ashley, she sat at their table at lunch? That she was, more or less, an Ashley herself?

There was no way she could walk into the refectory in the company of Sadie Graham. Ashley Spencer would choke on her fat-free soy chips if Sadie came within ten feet of their table.

"Hey, let's go," Sadie said, giving Lauren another wide, goofy smile. Lauren had forgotten how sweet-natured Sadie was. And this was her first day back after three years away. How could Lauren give Sadie the brush-off and let her eat by herself while Lauren sat with her new, über-uppity friends?

They started walking together down the long corridor toward the refectory. One thing was sure: Today they couldn't all eat lunch together. If Lauren walked up to the Ashleys with Sadie in tow, looking all owl-faced and frumpy, they'd turn their backs on her—on *Lauren*.

All her hard work this semester infiltrating their ranks would be for nothing. She'd be off Ashley's birthday party guest list quicker than you could say "Funyun-breath fatty." And then Lauren would never be able to destroy them. They'd do all they could to destroy *her*. The refectory door loomed.

They were steps away. . . .

She had to do something. . . .

"You know what?" Lauren said, turning quickly to Sadie and speaking much too fast. "I really feel like a Gino's sandwich today. You want to?"

Sadie looked doubtful. "Gino's? Are we allowed?"

"Sure," Lauren lied. Gino's was an Italian deli a few blocks away that was a popular after-school hangout. School policy restricted off-campus privileges to the eighth graders alone. But Lauren would risk getting an infraction and late study hall for this. If they got caught, maybe that little lie she'd told Christian earlier would come true after all. Funny how that happens.

Sadie's hand hovered over the door handle, and it looked as if Lauren would have no choice but to enter the refectory with her old friend. But after a few moments, Sadie shrugged. "Sure. Gino's it is."

7

IT'S HER PARTY AND SHE'LL
FREAK IF SHE WANTS TO

T WAS THURSDAY AFTERNOON AND SCHOOL WAS
over, thank goodness, for the day. Ashley Spencer
wandered into the sunroom of her family's palatial
home, gazing idly out at San Francisco Bay and wondering
if it was still warm enough for a spot of sailing. She hadn't
taken her cute little Sunfish out for ages. There was just
way too much to think about right now.

Princess Dahlia von Fluffsterhaus, the Spencers'
labradoodle puppy, scampered into the room, and Ashley
scooped her up, stroking the puppy's silky curls. In the week
since their visit to Mona Mazur's mint-colored house, Ashley
and her mother had made a little progress planning her
Super-Sweet Thirteen on December ninth. Mona had come
over on Saturday to show sketches and discuss menu ideas,

plus go over dull things like budgets. As if how much anything cost mattered!

Mona had sat right there, on the cream-colored sofa in the sunroom, sketches and plans and photographs spread all over the slab-granite coffee table, and talked about the circus theme.

Ashley lapped up every word of it. All her worries that the circus theme was going to be too babyish and immature were dispelled once Mona started describing her vision. The house was going to be turned into a giant big top, with red and white canvas draping the ceiling. Fire-eaters on stilts would line the front path as guests arrived. A master of ceremonies wearing a black tailcoat and brandishing a whip would welcome everyone at the door. A swing would dangle from the mezzanine floor, so acrobats from Cirque du Soleil could fly through the air above everyone's heads.

In the main living room, inside a huge vintage lion's cage, the burlesque rockabilly band the StripHall Queens would perform, while the food would be served by gymnasts in glittery leotards riding unicycles. And her grand entrance would be on a Vespa painted with tiger stripes. She'd be dressed in a shiny, skintight acrobat's outfit, she decided—at least for that portion of the evening, anyway. Ashley knew she'd have to change at least five times throughout the party. Hello! She couldn't just wear one color all night. It was her party, after all.

Ashley flopped onto the sofa and closed her eyes, Dahlia von Fluffsterhaus curled up in the crook of her arm. She could see it all now—the swooping spotlights, the glamorous acrobats, the speechless guests. The invitations to this party were going to be the hottest tickets in town. It was going to be the best day of her life. Until her birthday party next year, of course.

All the girls at Miss Gamble's would be clawing their eyes out to get invited. Too bad—not everybody could come! Especially not that little dork Sadie Graham, who had recently returned from the East Coast. Ashley had harbored a grudge against that girl ever since fourth grade, when Sadie had spread the rumor that Ashley was born a boy. For a harrowing few days, everyone called her "Ash-*he*" and snickered behind her back.

The rumor was sort of based on reality—Sadie's dad was Ashley's mom's doctor, and when Ashley was born, he'd mistakenly checked the wrong box for gender. All her old hospital pictures had her wearing blue caps and blue onesies on the first day. Ashley had wrought her revenge by telling everyone she'd seen Sadie picking her nose and eating its contents. So maybe "Boogers" as a nickname wasn't too creative, but it did the trick.

Now that she was thinking about it, Ashley vaguely remembered that Lauren had once been Sadie's partner in crime. Had it actually been Lauren who'd come up with the she-man nickname? Whatever. That was all in the past. Lauren was one of them now. Even though the girl had skipped out on lunch with them three times in a row that week. Lauren had explained that she was missing lunch because she had a bunch of dentist appointments. Something to do with a loose filling and too much kissing—too much information, in Ashley's opinion.

Lili had mentioned she thought she'd seen Lauren sneaking off campus with her old friend, but Ashley completely dismissed the idea. Why would Lauren hang out with a wet rag like Sadie when she was one of the Ashleys now? Lili must have been seeing things. Besides, Lauren was a total goody-goody. She'd never do something as daring as break the rules. The girl was never even out of uniform.

"Hey, honey." Her mother's voice interrupted Ashley's train of thought. Matilda plumped down at the other end of the sofa, resting one soft hand on Ashley's feet. "I feel like lying down myself."

"You're still not feeling well?" Ashley opened her eyes and looked over at her mother. Matilda was really not her usual beautiful, serene self. She was all bundled up in an eco-chic Linda Loudermilk sweater and loose Juicy sweatpants, a pair of angora socks swaddling her narrow feet. Her face was wan and splotchy, and she kept pushing her hair back from her face as though it was bothering her.

"Not really," said Matilda, squeezing Ashley's cashmere-covered toes. She gave a deep sigh. "I'm sorry—I know it's a drag for you. I just feel so tired and run-down. And the thought of doing any painting makes me feel sick."

"That's too bad," Ashley sympathized, though she was secretly relieved about the painting bit. This wasn't a good time for her mother to be locked up in her studio painting her bizarre pictures of writhing Technicolor women. They had a major event to plan. Even with Mona Mazur in charge, there was still a ton to do. They hadn't even decided on the invitations yet, or auditioned any of the unicycle-riding gymnasts.

"Ash, I've been thinking." Her mother sounded all dreamy and distant. "How would you feel if we decided to scale the party down a little? It's just, I'm so under the weather right now, and your dad and I were talking—he'd kind of prefer a smaller, family thing as well."

Ashley sat bolt upright, spilling Dahlia von Fluffsterhaus onto the rug. The afternoon sun pouring through the plate glass suddenly made *her* feel sick too. Had she fallen asleep? Was this some kind of nightmare?

"You know," her mother was saying, "it would still be a lovely party. Chef could make all your favorite food. We'd hire that great DJ we met at the art museum benefit, and you could have a few friends here. We'd just roll back the carpet in the living room and turn it into a dance floor, and we could use this room to store all your gifts. It'd be fun and festive. What do you say?"

Ashley swallowed hard. She wasn't sure whether to laugh, cry, or scream. A DJ? A few friends? Rolling back the carpet? *Fun and festive*? What was this—some bad teen movie where kids danced next to lampshades and puked on the Oriental rugs?

"But Mom," she pleaded. "I've already told everyone about *everything*. Like the Vespa, and the acrobats, and the StripHall Queens! Everyone at Miss Gamble's knows every detail. If we change it now, it'll look like I was lying! Or even worse—like we can't afford it!"

Matilda sighed deeply and shook her head.

"Oh, Ashley," she said. "It doesn't matter what other people think. I'm telling you that I don't feel up to having some big gang of people take over the house and turn it upside down for days on end."

"But it's just NOT FAIR!" shrieked Ashley, totally losing her composure and feeling like stamping her feet in distress. "Don't you even care about how I feel? Just a little bit?"

"Darling, don't be that way, you'll still have a lovely party," her mother said firmly.

"No, I won't!" Ashley started hyperventilating. This was the worst possible thing her mother could have said to her. This was even worse than the time her parents told her she was too young to fly to Bali with them. It was even worse than the time they put a stop on her credit card.

Her birthday was over before it even began! "It's all or nothing. If I can't have the party you promised me, I don't want any party at all!"

Matilda gave another long sigh, then slowly stood up. She turned to face Ashley, hands on svelte hips.

"Okay, then, if that's what you want. You'll have no party at all."

What—no party? Her mother looked serious. Ashley was incensed.

"That's really not funny, Mom."

"That's because it's not a joke. You say it's all or nothing—well, I guess it has to be nothing then. End of discussion."

And with that, Matilda left the room.

Ashley sat for a while, tears forming in her eyes, fuming as she listened to her mother's footsteps plodding up the stairs. How dare Matilda casually decimate her life like this? She reached for her puppy, but Dahlia von Fluffsterhaus had already wandered off, annoyed at getting pushed off the sofa.

So instead Ashley grabbed an Indian silk cushion and hugged it, squeezing it so hard she thought the stuffing might pop out. A few minutes later she heard her father playing the guitar, picking out some dinky folk tune her mother liked—he was always playing to her these days, because she said it made her feel more relaxed and centered. Whatever! What about their own daughter and her shattered life? Nobody in this house cared one iota.

That was it. Ashley just had to get out of the House of Horrors. She picked up the sneakers she'd cast off earlier, stomped over to jerk open the French doors, and made sure she slammed them as loudly as possible on her way out. At the bottom of the terraced garden was a pathway that wound all the way to the marina. After ten minutes of good, angry stomping, complete with intermittent sobs and occasional petulant squeaks, Ashley was there.

Even the weather didn't care about her terrible situation. It was still sunny, the breeze light and playful. Maybe she'd take out her Sunfish after all and whiz around on the bouncing waves for a while. She was supposed to tell her parents or a member of the staff whenever she was planning to sail, but Ashley didn't care. They didn't care about *her*, anyway. They'd probably be happy if she drowned or sailed off forever to some faraway island where the natives were cannibals.

She walked along one of the bobbing docks lined with large, pristine white yachts till she reached her parents', the *Matilda*, where her own little boat was tied up. How typical of her father to name the boat after his wife rather than his only daughter! Message to Ashley: *They don't really love you.*

Ashley crouched and began unwinding the Sunfish's

rope, wishing she had a jet-setting model mom like A.A., who let her daughter do whatever she wanted. Or strict, hyper parents like Lili's, who would never, ever go back on their word. Or even Lauren's new-money parents, who at least grasped the importance of showing off your wealth. Instead she was stuck with selfish richie-rich hippies who were so busy being in love with each other they forgot what really mattered in life. Like the fact that their only daughter was turning thirteen!

"Hey—you might not want to go out right now. The weather's about to turn." A boy's voice, sounding like it came from under the docks, made her jump out of her skin. Ashley lost her grip on the rope she was picking at and plopped down hard on her butt.

"Excuse me?" she squeaked, hoping she hadn't embarrassed herself with that little tumble. A head appeared over the nearby ship railing—it was a boy with dark hair, a crinkly smile, and a nut-brown tan—a total stud.

"Sorry to startle you." He grinned and stepped down from his boat. He was tall, around her age, dressed in faded jeans, Nike vintage sneakers, and a blue cotton sweater. "I'm Cooper."

"Ashley." She clambered to her feet, out of breath from all that marching along the path, not to mention the fright from hearing a voice from nowhere.

"I was just doing some barnacle scraping," he explained, gesturing at the boat moored next to the *Matilda*. It was even bigger, a brilliant white with the name *Flown the Coop* spelled out in large red letters. At least Cooper's parents cared enough to name their yacht after *him*! "I saw you getting ready to go out on the Sunfish, and . . . uh, sorry if I startled you, but it's going to get real choppy in a minute. You don't want to get out there and . . . you know." He made a motion with his hands that indicated a capsized boat.

"Oh yeah." Ashley waved her hand at him like it was no big deal. "Thanks for the warning."

"Anytime," he said.

Ashley put her hands on her hips and looked put out. "I wish the weather wasn't so bad. I was really looking forward to getting out there today."

"It was nice earlier. Where were you?" he asked teasingly, eyes sparkling. God, he was cute! Why hadn't she ever met him before?

"With my stupid mom." Ashley felt a bit self-conscious talking about her problems, but she was disappointed that she wasn't going to get out to the ocean, and she felt like venting.

Cooper nodded. "You guys fought?"

"A little." Ashley shook her head. "I just hate my parents sometimes." Maybe complaining about your family wasn't the best way to attract a guy, but Ashley just needed someone to talk to at the moment.

"My parents can get kind of annoying too. And I don't even see my mom that often," he told her, a wistful note in his voice.

Ashley nodded, idly watching the seagulls duck and dive into the water. His parents were probably just like hers, too rich to care. "I was looking forward to getting away for a little bit," she announced a tad melodramatically. "Don't you feel like everything"—she gestured to indicate the entire bay in front of them—"is just too much sometimes?"

"Totally." He smiled again and started ambling away down the dock. "Take care," he called.

She was looking at the lighthouse in the far distance and didn't notice he was leaving. "Wait a sec!" she cried. She wasn't letting Mr. Yacht Club Hottie make his escape *that* easily. "Do you . . . do you live near here or something?"

"Yup." Cooper nodded, pointing in the opposite direction from Ashley's house.

"I was just thinking," said Ashley, feeling nervous all of a sudden. And when was she ever nervous around boys? She made boys nervous, not the other way around. "I mean—I don't even know if you're free or whatever. But I'm, like, having a party? For my birthday? Would you like to—I mean, it's in a couple of weeks. The party, I mean." What was wrong with her? Why was she talking like that—making everything a question when it was a statement and not being able to ask the question she did want to ask?

But she needn't have worried. Cooper seemed to get the gist. "Sure." He nodded.

It was only after Cooper had flashed his dazzling smile again, only after he'd loped off into the sunset, only after Ashley finished retying the Sunfish's rope and started making her way back through the marina, that she remembered one crucial point.

Her party was canceled.

Huh. So maybe she would have to go back home and tell her mother that after much careful consideration, the smaller, more intimate gathering Matilda had proposed was acceptable after all. So maybe there would be no tigers jumping through hoops, no crowd-pleasing entrance on a Vespa, no seven-foot-tall big-top birthday cake.

But maybe there would be something better. One very important, very handsome guest.

You couldn't invite a guy to a party if there wasn't one, could you?

8

IS IT BIRTH-DAY OR BIRTH-WEEK? FOR THE ASHLEYS ONE CELEBRATION IS NEVER ENOUGH

ILI PUSHED OPEN THE GLASS DOOR OF BLOWFISH Sushi and beamed at the black-clad hostess. This was more like it—no crummy diners *this* weekend; no unpleasant posers from inferior schools, either. Max was a sweetheart, but sometimes Lili had some serious doubts about his taste. He would probably think Blowfish Sushi was overly trendy and pretentious. But what Max thought didn't really matter. Not on this particular Sunday night, anyway.

"I have a reservation for four," Lili told the hostess. "Under Ashley Li."

"One of your party is already here, Miss Li." The girl was

wearing a really cute mini and gladiator sandals. When Lili grew up, she was going to run her own nightclub, and this was *just* the kind of outfit she'd wear as she cruised the place every evening, making sure everything was perfect. "Please follow me."

Lili spotted A.A. at the Ashleys' favorite table near the back of the restaurant, close to the black-lacquered sushi bar with its reed-seat bar stools and giant exotic fish tank. This restaurant had the Ashleys' SOA, so it was the perfect choice for one of their ritual events—the prebirthday gift exchange. It was a school night, but even her uptight parents understood the importance of such an event and made an exception.

"Hi, pretty!" Lili called, dropping her mother-of-pearl evening bag into the nearest empty chair and stretching to air kiss A.A. Even sitting down, A.A. looked long and lean in a black silk L.A.M.B. jumpsuit that probably looked good on only two people in the world—Gwen Stefani and A.A.

"Hey, pretty!" A.A. responded. "I love that color on you."

"Thanks." Lili knew this wasn't just flattery—she loved her new outfit. She'd convinced her mother to take her to New York last weekend, and Lili had scored a hot Thakoon dress, right out of the showroom.

"Hey, guys!"

They looked up to see Lauren making a beeline for the table, followed by a boy carrying a gigantic gold box with a huge red bow on it.

"Hi, pretty!" A.A. and Lili chorused, making Lauren turn pink. Lili leaned over to kiss her on both cheeks— without touching, of course, because nobody wanted red lip smudges all over their face. Lauren was so eager to be greeted that she bumped noses with A.A.

Lili wasn't sure if it was touching or pathetic, the way Lauren still wasn't comfortable with being an Ashley. Maybe it wasn't *that* surprising. Lauren was new to this game, while the other Ashleys had been queens of Miss Gamble's for years. Sometimes it felt like they'd been *born* into royalty.

"You guys all know Christian, right?" Lauren asked, blushing more deeply as she introduced tall, blond, and handsome standing next to her, who put the gift on an empty chair.

"Oh yeah, we met at Lauren's last week, right?" A.A. asked pleasantly.

But Christian looked confused. "I don't think so," he said with a puzzled smile.

"No, we totally met—you and Lauren had just come back from . . ." A.A.'s voice trailed off, as it was only then that she noticed that behind him, Lauren was shaking her head so vigorously her earrings were in danger of falling off.

Lili tried to hide a smile. Obviously A.A. was thinking of Lauren's other boyfriend. She sized up Christian from head to toe. She'd met Alex the other week, and this one was definitely a looker too. That girl sure got around.

61

Lauren kissed her boyfriend good-bye and sat down next to Lili. "Is Ashley here yet?" she asked.

Tonight they'd present Ashley with her Big Gift, saving smaller presents for her actual birthday and a third round of gifts for the night of her party. This tradition had been established in fifth grade, and the only thing different this year was the fact that Lauren was there. Lauren was so thrilled to be included that she'd volunteered to pick up Ashley's birthday gift herself.

Lili thought Lauren was probably trying to make up for the fact that she'd been totally flaky lately—she hardly joined them for lunch anymore and seemed to have some kind of meeting, appointment, or extra class every day. And just yesterday she'd practically run away when Lili saw her at Gino's. Lili had gotten a special dispensation to go off campus to get doughnuts for the Honor Board meeting. She'd been surprised to see Lauren there, and even more surprised when Lauren booked as fast as she could in the other direction. What was going on with that girl? It wasn't as if Lili was going to slap her with a demerit. They were friends.

"You'd better sign the card," A.A. reminded her as Lili settled into her seat, tucking the tiny evening bag behind the small of her back, the way her mother always did. "Ashley'll be here any minute."

"I had it designed exactly as you specified," Lauren told

Lili, producing a thick marbled envelope from the shopping bag at her feet.

"You went to the Venetian place?" Lili scrutinized the envelope. This was the first time she'd handed this task over to someone else. "You asked for the handmade paper?"

Lauren nodded, her long sleek, chestnut hair swinging.

"And I asked them to use thirteen different colors in the marbling, because it's Ashley's thirteenth birthday." Lauren beamed. Then her face fell.

Lili looked around. What was up? At the doorway was a girl from school, one of those nobodies—Sadie something, who'd recently returned from wherever . . . oh yeah, Lili remembered now. "Check it out! Isn't that Boogers Graham?" Lili nudged A.A. and smirked.

"Oh, hush." A.A. laughed.

Lauren didn't join in the laughter and stared at Sadie with a shocked expression.

A.A. peered at Sadie more closely. "You know what, she looks different."

"Yeah, out of our awful uniform she actually looks normal," Lili conceded. The Ashleys had discovered that the key to looking good was to accessorize the uniform to the extreme, so that it was forced to look flattering. Wearing a simple black top and blue jeans, with her hair pulled back, did wonders for Sadie's looks.

Sadie was about to leave the restaurant with her family but turned around and stared at their table intently. Then she began heading their way.

"I've, uh—I've got to go to the bathroom!" Lauren declared, pushing her way past Lili and hurrying to the ladies'.

When Sadie arrived at their table, she looked confused.

"Can we help you?" Lili asked, not trying to be rude, but seriously, who invited her?

"No." Sadie shook her head. She looked at Lauren's empty seat and blinked. "Huh."

Lili and A.A. exchanged shrugs as Sadie walked away. Lauren returned to their table after what seemed like an inordinately long time.

A.A. took a sip of virgin sake from a tiny, cerulean blue cup. "Hurry up, Lili—she's here!"

Lili capped the gold pen Lauren had handed her and quickly returned the card to its envelope. Sure enough, Ashley was sashaying toward them, looking like a streak of gold herself. Her blond hair was loose, apart from one long braid wound around her head like a band, interwoven with a filmy gold ribbon. She wore a layered, Grecian-style silk dress, which she informed them was vintage, and Halston. She must have spent all day getting ready—no wonder she'd skipped school that day.

"My mother met Rachel Zoe at a celebrity fashion benefit last month," Ashley told them after the obligatory double kisses. "And Rachel told her this look would be perfect for me."

"She was right." A.A. grinned.

"You look like a movie star," Lauren agreed.

Lili had to stop herself from rolling her eyes. Why did A.A. and Lauren always have to be such kiss-asses when Ashley was around? Had they forgotten about AshleyRank already? Maybe Lili should remind them who was currently wearing the crown.

She picked up the giant box wedged into Ashley's seat and lifted it onto the table, Lauren quickly moving the delicate sake cups out of the way.

"For me?" gasped Ashley, feigning surprise. She slipped into her seat and thrummed the box with her gold-tipped fingernails.

"I brought this with me," Lauren said, offering her a ceramic letter opener, "so you can look at your card without getting your nails dirty."

"So sweet!" Ashley was certainly in a friendly mood tonight. Lili was amazed by how long she spent looking at the card, counting the different colors in the delicate marbling and reading the calligraphy message ("To the fairest of them all") aloud several times. This was kind of strange: Usually

Ashley dispensed with the card in ten seconds because she couldn't wait to rip her gift open.

"Don't you want to see what's in the box?" A.A. asked. Her puzzled expression suggested that she was surprised as well. Was this the new, modest, number-four-with-a-bullet Ashley?

"Sure." Ashley sighed, carefully slitting through the packaging with the ceramic opener. Lili couldn't wait to see her face when she opened the box. Lauren may have collected the present from Neiman Marcus, but it was Lili's idea, and Lili was the one who'd called the store with specific instructions.

"You're going to love it," Lauren told her.

Ashley peeled back the layers of marbled tissue paper, and her eyes widened.

"How . . . how *apropos*!" She reached her hands into the box and pulled out a golden helmet, the initial *A* picked out in crystals.

"It's for your Vespa!" A.A. cheered. They all knew exactly what Ashley was getting for her birthday.

"It's Chanel!" Lauren added. "Special order!"

"I love it," said Ashley, holding it up to her face and smiling. Lili gave her a sidelong look: Ashley was certainly quite subdued tonight. Normally she had one of two reactions to a gift.

If she didn't like it—because it wasn't what she was expecting, or the item in question was no longer sufficiently "it," or she'd just seen a picture of someone like Chauncey Raven, the beleaguered pop star who'd recently lost custody of her two kids, with the exact same thing—Ashley would usually make a pouty face, thank them in a faint, pained voice, and put the present away in its box or bag immediately.

If she loved the gift—because it was what she'd told them to buy, or because she'd just seen a picture of someone like Sloan Hess, the way-too-hip and way-too-skinny British supermodel with the exact same thing—then she would shriek with joy and make sure the whole restaurant could see it. But tonight she was doing neither of these things. She was just acting like a normal person does when they get a gift. And this made Lili deeply, deeply suspicious. Something *had* to be going on.

"So what's the deal with all the party arrangements?" A.A. asked, after Ashley had finally stowed the helmet in its box under her seat and a platter with an extra-long dragon roll (made with thirteen ingredients, as Lauren took pains to point out) had been placed on the table between them.

"Oh, you know," said Ashley, blithely gesturing with her chopsticks. "Mona Mazur is taking care of pretty much everything."

"What have you decided about the unicyclists' costumes?"

Lauren asked. They'd discussed this at length just a few lunchtimes ago, but Lauren had missed the whole conversation: She'd felt faint on the way into the refectory and had to spend lunchtime lying in a darkened room in the sick bay. Just another lunchtime powwow she'd missed that week. No wonder she was so behind the curve.

"Oh, you know. Whatever." Ashley nibbled at the piece of dragon roll squished between her chopsticks. "I've been meaning to tell you all—I met the cutest boy down at the marina yesterday after school. His name is Cooper, and he's totally adorable. And he was totally into me!"

"Did you invite him to the party?" A.A. wanted to know.

Ashley nodded. "Uh-huh. And he's tall, so much taller than Tri."

"That wouldn't be hard." A.A. snorted.

"How old is he?" Lauren took a giant bite of dragon roll, half the rice spilling onto the tablecloth.

"He looks like he's our age. I forgot to ask him which school he goes to—duh!"

Lili toyed with the food on her square black plate, expertly lifting a stray slice of ginger with her chopsticks. Ashley was gushing on about this new guy but seemed very reluctant to talk about the party, which was unlike her. That wasn't the only uncharacteristic trait she was displaying that evening.

"What do you think?" Ashley asked, showing them a sample of the party invitations. She didn't meet Lili's eyes as she held up the piece of paper.

"They're so cute!" said Lili, trying to hide her surprise. She was telling the truth: The invitations were chic—very graphic and fifties, with silhouetted figures dancing around an old record player. She noticed that Ashley had bought them from Kate's Paperie, and the cards were made from beautiful textured paper with embossed seals for each envelope.

Ashley had fantastic taste—nobody could ever dispute that. But considering all the over-the-top plans for the party Ashley had been talking about for the last two weeks, Lili thought the invitations would be much more special. She was expecting something amazing and custom-made, not a box of ready-made cards. They didn't even have a circus theme!

"So what are the StripHall Queens like?" Lauren asked, taking a sip from her citrusy "gin and tonic" (the gin a dash of ginger ale). "Did you get to meet them yet?"

"And is Cirque du Soleil going to perform 'Zumanity' or 'O'?" A.A. wanted to know.

Ashley looked momentarily flustered, but before she could answer their questions, all the lights in the restaurant went dark, and the speakers started playing a grand orchestral theme, interspersed with the StripHall Queens' latest hit,

"Lick Me! Eat Me! I'm Your Cake!" A whizzing, sparkling, glittering confection was brought over to their table.

The cake was made up of a towering ball of pink cotton candy, decorated with thirteen sparklers. It looked like a gorgeous pink bomb. On cue, Lili led the Ashleys in their version of "Happy Birthday." ("Happy Birthday to you. You belong at Nobu. With Mary-Kate and Ashley, and Lindsay Lohan, too.")

"Happy Birthday, pretty," Lili said, reaching over to give Ashley a huge hug and kiss. Okay, so maybe she sometimes hated Ashley a little bit for always having to be numero uno, even when certain blogs had decreed otherwise, but it was her birthday, and Ashley was still her best friend. When all was said and done, she loved the biatch.

"Make a wish!" A.A. urged, while Lauren took too many pictures with her digital camera.

Ashley closed her eyes and blew out the flames. When she opened her eyes, they were sparkling. "You guys are the best!"

Lili sighed. Ashley deserved everything that was coming to her.

9

THAT'S THE PROBLEM WITH OLD FRIENDS: THEY WANT TO DO THE SAME OLD THINGS

AUREN LOOKED OVER HER SHOULDER. EVER SINCE
Sadie had come back to Miss Gamble's, she'd been
developing neck strain from looking around all
the time to watch out for the Ashleys. School had let out
for the day, and Sadie had insisted they hang out after
school like they'd always done before. Sadie wanted to see
the famous Page mansion and wouldn't take any of
Lauren's excuses.

Bad luck for Lauren: It was the very day the Ashleys were
planning a huge shopping trip to prepare for Ashley's party.
Try as she might, Lauren couldn't dissuade her old friend, so
she'd begged off the retail rampage by saying her mom
wanted her to come home and help choose a color scheme
for the new wing.

Of course, so that she wouldn't blow her cover with the Ashleys, she had to get Sadie in the car, and out of sight, as soon as possible. Now where was Dex? You'd think some guy who didn't have much to do other than drive her around would be on time for once.

Lauren craned her neck toward the street, willing the Bentley to appear, and then stretched the opposite direction at the school gates to watch out for the Ashleys again.

"Why do you keep looking over there?" Sadie asked.

Lauren didn't answer, feeling a cold stab of fear when she saw a glint of Ashley's new Cartier bracelet in the sun. The three girls were walking past the playground and would be right at the front gates in a second. She'd be caught with Sadie! If only—

"Dex!"

The silver Bentley crested the hill, and Lauren grabbed Sadie's hand and led her to the car. She bundled Sadie into the backseat just as the Ashleys appeared. Lauren slammed the door. "Let's go!"

"What's the rush?" Dex asked, annoyed. "Easy on the hardware, okay, Page?"

If Sadie was annoyed at being rushed inside the car, she didn't show it. She was too busy staring at Dex. If possible, Dex was even cuter when he frowned. He wasn't Lauren's type in any way—he was way too old and too much of a brother figure for anything like *that* to come into play—but she could see the effect he had on everyone else she knew.

She suspected A.A. had had a major crush on him earlier this semester. Guinevere Parker had even asked Lauren if she could interview him for the school newspaper, part of some bogus feature on parking issues during rush hour in Nob Hill.

"Who *is* he?" Sadie whispered, pinching Lauren. "He's gorgeous!"

Lauren rolled her eyes, noticing how Sadie was staring at Dex almost as if she were hypnotized. "Dex, this is my friend Sadie. Sadie, this is Dex. He's my driver. And my father's intern, computer genius . . . whatever."

"Hey, sexy Sadie," Dex teased from the front seat, making Sadie squirm with delight.

"Does he have a girlfriend?" Sadie asked, when they'd arrived at the Pages' house and exited the car.

"Um, yes. And she's, like, ten years older than us," Lauren told her. She was a little annoyed at Sadie for insisting that they hang out on today of all days. Hadn't Lauren given up sitting at the most important table at lunch every day just for her? Sure, Sadie didn't know that, but the fact didn't make Lauren any less grumpy.

Hanging out with Sadie was just like before. But Lauren was twelve now, not nine. She didn't want to do all those things they used to do. Lauren thought longingly of the shopping trip she was currently missing. So maybe the whole time Ashley would hog all the best clothes and monopolize the salesclerks, but they were sure to all get coordinated outfits for the party, and she would be left out again.

Oh well. Too late now. This afternoon was all about Sadie.

"Sadie! Welcome back!" Trudy Page stood at the front double doors, a glass of freshly squeezed pomegranate juice in each hand. It would have been better if Lauren's mother hadn't coordinated her Cavalli outfit to match the pomegranate juice, because Sadie looked a little afraid of the vision in bright red waiting for them when they walked up the stone slab steps.

Not for the first time since she'd been allowed to join the Ashleys, Lauren felt an unwelcome twinge of embarrassment about her mother's fashion sense, followed by a flood of guilt. Her mother meant so well and only wanted Lauren to be happy. Trudy just hadn't got over the thrill of being super rich yet; it wasn't her fault, really. All she needed was a few friends like the Ashleys to get her on track and tell her what not to buy.

Oops. Did Lauren actually think of the Ashleys as her friends? This double-agent thing was getting a little more complicated than she'd thought.

"Sweetie, it's so good to see you again," Trudy said, ushering an openmouthed Sadie into their vast, airy house. It was all giant panes of glass and minimalist midcentury modern furniture in front, but Mediterranean-style in the back, complete with a pillared courtyard, where the house faced the city's most exclusive marina.

Sergei, her ex-academic father, had requested a traditional den-slash-library, and her mother had the brainwave of decorating it like a Scottish baronial lodge, using old (i.e., last season's) beige Burberry trenches for the curtains and disks cut from two-hundred-year-old Scotch bottles to build a stained-glass coffee table. But Lauren's favorite room was the chill-out zone at the top of the house, just beneath the helipad, where the walls were white, the only furniture was oversize chocolate leather beanbags, and the controls for the Bose stereo system were hidden in the bleached ash floor planks.

She led her old friend along three of the house's long, slate-floored corridors to her bedroom, Sadie trailing behind like an eager puppy.

"I've never seen a house like this," Sadie gushed, her green plaid uniform looking more awkward and ill-fitting than ever. Really, Sadie was as awkward and ill-fitting as her clothes. "You guys really hit it big!"

Lauren cringed a little and wished Sadie wasn't so blunt.

Sadie wandered around Lauren's two-story bedroom with her pale blue eyes almost bulging out of her head. She plopped onto Lauren's king-size feather bed, bouncing up and down like a little kid and then springing up again to run over to the mirrored closets that lined the room's long back wall.

"It's like a . . . it's like a palace!" she squealed, gazing at her reflection in one of the mirrored doors. "What's upstairs?"

"Oh, just . . . you know." Lauren shrugged. She liked her room and was still kind of amazed by it herself, but there was something seriously uncool about Sadie's kid-in-the-candy-store reaction.

"You could have a whole family living up here!" Sadie had clomped up the circular staircase to the loft sleep-and-play area. "Omigod! You really could—there are, like, four beds up here!"

Lauren decided it wasn't time to tell Sadie about the all-Ashley sleepover earlier in the semester, the reason Trudy had had the four red-cedar bunks specially built. Anyway, Sadie was distracted by the matching cubbies packed with books, toys, and games.

"Can we play something? Do you have Monopoly?"

"No." Lauren felt herself frowning. This wasn't good. Sadie was getting distracted by all the childish stuff. Why didn't she want to go through Lauren's closet, like any normal, self-respecting seventh grader? Maybe Sadie needed a nudge in the right direction. "Do you want to try on some of my shoes? I think we're around the same size, and I have, like, four dozen pairs. Some are still in their boxes."

Sadie's face fell. "Can't we play some games? I hate shoe shopping. My mother has to *make* me go at the start of every school year, and I'm still getting over that."

"I know—how about a spa makeover? You should see my bathroom." Lauren headed off down the stairs, hoping Sadie would follow.

Her phone began to buzz. Lauren picked it up hopefully. Maybe one of the Ashleys had some juicy gossip. Maybe Lili was calling to dish about why Ashley was being oh-so-mysterious about her party, or A.A. was calling to complain about Lili's crazy camping plan. Maybe it was Ashley herself, calling to thank Lauren, yet again, for picking up the fabulous gift.

Anything but Sadie, romping around upstairs like a little girl in a toy store. Lauren made a mental note to give those games, most of them still shrink-wrapped and brand-new, to charity.

"Hello?" Lauren answered. It was Ashley, calling to find out if she was done with her mom and if she could meet them at the boutique *tout de suite*.

"You're missing all the fun," Ashley cooed.

Maybe Ashley just wanted a bigger audience as she tried on her five outfits. Maybe she just wanted someone else to tell her she looked wonderful in everything she put on. It didn't matter.

Lauren shut off her phone and made a quick decision. She turned to Sadie, with the too-sweet smile she'd seen Ashley give people when she wanted them to do something she knew they didn't want to do.

"Listen, that was my dad, and I kind of forgot I promised him I would go pick up something for my mom that he ordered at Graff's." God, it was so easy to lie when you got into the habit!

"Really?" Sadie asked, looking completely disappointed. "But I brought Felicity!" she said, pulling out a much-loved California Girl doll from her oversized bag.

"Next time, I promise." Then she said the magic words that were sure to squelch any more protests from Sadie. "And don't worry, Dex can drive you home."

10

A.A. DISCOVERS THE WISDOM
THAT IS BEYONCÉ

A.A. DIDN'T MIND PLAYING SOCCER IN THE rain and mud, but on a wet afternoon like this, most of the other girls in her ad hoc league made their excuses and didn't show up to the game at the Jackson Playground. Normally this would get on her nerves, but as it turned out, she had something else to do anyway.

Last night at dinner, Lili had talked Ashley into a shopping trip after school for her birthday party outfits. Lili had argued that the Ashleys needed to do this together so they could make sure all their outfits coordinated without clashing. Plus, Ashley had been talking for ages about needing five different dresses. It was only a few weeks till the party. They needed to start shopping *now*.

Ashley had been a little reluctant at first, which was unexpected. Lili was right, Ashley was acting a bit odd about her party. But once they hit the shops, Ashley soon regained her shopaholic form.

They'd changed out of their uniforms at school and were downtown by three thirty, and by four A.A. was tired of trying on clothes. The other girls never seemed to weary of this, but they were way more indecisive than A.A.—she'd found a great dress in the first twenty minutes! A hot pink number with a leopard print—kind of out there for her, but A.A. liked how loud it was. Her mother always said there was nothing more boring than good taste.

So now she was slumped on an ivory suede sofa, sending IMs, listening to the thumping in-store soundtrack, and watching Ashley and Lili wander in and out of changing rooms, asking her opinion.

She turned her attention to her iPhone. New IM: Ned wanted her to come home. He'd just bought the latest version of Dark Void for his Wii, something he'd been obsessing about all week. A.A. sighed—she had a different kind of obsessing to deal with right now, and that was the Ashley vs. Lili fashion smackdown, round five hundred sixty-four.

Those two had never seen an outfit they didn't want to rip off each other's back and claim as their own. They both emerged simultaneously from their respective changing rooms, leaving A.A. to act—as usual—as fashion referee.

"That's way too similar to this dress," Ashley told Lili, frowning at Lili's cascading ruffles. "You don't want to look like a copycat, do you?"

"But chocolate brown looks so much more striking on me, don't you think, A.A.?" Ever since her number-one rating on AshleyRank, Lili wasn't going down without a fight.

"I think the dresses are pretty different," A.A. said, but she could tell Ashley wasn't convinced. Ashley picked at the ruching on her dress, a discontented look clouding her face. "And anyway, Ash—you're only going to wear this for half an hour, right? It doesn't matter if it *kind of* looks like Lili's dress."

"Actually, it *kind of* does," snapped Ashley. She stood on her tiptoes and stared at her reflection in the full-length gilt mirror propped against one wall. "It's my party, after all!"

"Yeah," said Lili with a sigh, bunching her jet-black hair into a ponytail and twisting in front of the mirror, checking out the neckline of her dress. "What's going on with the party, exactly? Any new developments?"

"No. Why, should there be?" Ashley turned on one stockinged foot and marched back into her changing room, yanking the velvet curtain shut.

Lili raised an eyebrow at A.A., as if to say, *I told you so*. On the way out of the restaurant last night, Lili had asked her if she'd noticed anything odd about Ashley's behavior. A.A. just shrugged, but now that she'd had time to think about it, maybe Lili was right.

Ashley was acting a little secretive. Maybe she was just sick of incessantly going over every detail of the party. Or maybe, more likely, she didn't want anyone to know some of the big surprises she had planned. Not even the other Ashleys. Huh! A.A. crossed her long legs and picked up her iPhone again. Let Ashley have her secrets. As long as one of them wasn't "Ashley and Tri get back together and start grossing everyone out with their lovey-dovey act," A.A. really didn't care.

Ashley re-emerged, peering out to make sure Lili wasn't hovering.

"What do you think?" Ashley asked, doing a mock catwalk stroll toward the mirror and then striking a pose. Her dress was a stunning turquoise blue, with a jeweled neckline. "Is this drop-dead gorgeous or what?"

"Omigod, it was made for you!" A loud, too-cheery voice announced that Lauren had arrived.

"What kept you?" Ashley demanded.

Lauren's laugh was shrill. She heaped her handbag and coat on the couch next to A.A. and began talking too fast. "Oh, you know—the decorator forgot to bring the right swatches, so it was a total mess . . ." But she stopped talking when she noticed that Ashley was no longer listening and had wandered over to the clothing racks across the room to check out the selection there.

A.A. wished Lauren wouldn't gush so much. She was one of the gang now—well, sort of, and maybe not forever. Although lately it seemed like Lauren was sort of schizo. At school she was either nowhere to be found or else clinging to them like a vine. Even so, Ashley had specifically invited her to the birthday dinner, and she'd made a point of calling Lauren every five minutes, begging her to meet them for shopping. Lauren didn't need to try this hard.

Ashley marched back in front of them with her hands on her hips, wearing a different dress.

"Red velvet," she mused, pursing her lips. "Like a red velvet rope. Super exclusive! What do you think?"

Lauren studied Ashley's reflection in the mirror carefully. A.A. thought the dress made Ashley look like a stop sign. Of course, Lauren dutifully obliged with a compliment. "I love it!"

"Ash, we can bring dates, right?" Lili asked, peeking out from behind the curtain. "I already told Max about it."

"Of course!"

"Who are you going to bring?" A.A. asked Lauren.

"Oh God!" Lauren cried. "I hadn't even thought of that!"

A.A. looked bemused. "I don't know how you do it—dating two guys at once."

Lauren looked down at her hands. "It's awful, actually," she said. "I don't even know which one I like better. Have you ever had that problem?"

It took A.A. a moment to answer. She'd been thinking of Hunter, and how she did like him, and her mind had disturbingly wandered over to Tri. "No, I like Hunter," she announced, even though it wasn't an answer to Lauren's question.

Thankfully, Lauren dropped that line of questioning and turned to Ashley. "Have you thought about having a VIP area at your party?" she suggested, heading over to the racks to pick out some dresses.

"I was totally going to suggest that!" Lili wrenched back her dressing-room curtain, still zipping up her dress. It was rust-colored velvet, very similar in color and style to the one Ashley was wearing. A.A. tried to suppress a smile.

"Tsk!" Ashley sniffed. "Of course I've thought of that. Not only will there be a VIP area, there'll be a VIP dance floor. Only the Ashleys will be allowed to dance on *that*."

"With boys, right?" Lauren asked anxiously. The thought of boys made A.A. groan. She didn't even know if she wanted Hunter to come to this party, let alone dance with her in some VIP area while everybody else stood around staring. And then she felt guilty. Why didn't she want to dance with Hunter? It wasn't as though he was a lame loser like Tri.

"A.A.—hi!" A.A. couldn't believe it. Speak of the devil—or at least, the devil's girlfriend. Cecily, Tri's new squeeze, was waving at her from the other side of the store.

"Hey," said A.A., fluttering her fingers and wriggling down even farther into the sofa while Cecily deposited her umbrella in the stand by the door. She would rather watch Lili and Ashley have a tug-of-war with a velvet hair band right now than get into some "Tri is so great" conversation with his love-struck sweetheart.

Too late. Cecily was scurrying over, sitting down on the sofa next to A.A. and shaking drops of water out of her auburn bob. Cecily looked fresh and pretty in a plain T-shirt and dark-rinse jeans. A.A.'s phone vibrated.

"It's my brother," she told Cecily, checking the screen. "He just got the new version of Dark Void. That's a—"

"He's got it already? I thought it wouldn't be released until Tuesday." Cecily looked excited. "I can't wait to check it out. Hey, I was meaning to ask you—have you played that new soccer game yet? The FIFA 08? My dad just got it for me, and I love it. You play?"

A.A. nodded, saying nothing, vaguely aware that Ashley and Lili were now arguing in loud voices about who got to wear velvet at Ashley's party. She didn't want to like Cecily, but . . . she had to admit that the girl wasn't all that bad. She was a soccer jock like A.A., and clearly a total gamer as well.

She had a cool haircut and looked great in a pair of designer jeans, but she didn't seem like the kind of girl who spent all her time worrying about her appearance.

"Well, if you must know, it makes your legs look short," Ashley was saying to Lili.

"Really? I didn't want to say this, but something about that dress makes you look like a red velvet cupcake."

"Maybe you should both try on something else," Lauren wheedled, edging past them toward the changing room with a stack of dresses folded over her arm. A.A. rolled her eyes at Cecily, as though she wasn't with the bickering duo, and Cecily smiled. The speakers above her head started blasting out a Beyoncé song, and Cecily absentmindedly started singing along.

"I can have another you by tomorrow," she sang, tapping her fingers on the sofa. *"So don't you ever for a second get to thinking you're irreplaceable."*

Irreplaceable. Is that what A.A. used to think? That Tri would always be there, waiting for her to like him? What an idiot she'd been, hanging around after Tri kissed her, expecting him to end things with Ashley and ask her out! She was totally *replaceable*. Here was the living proof, sitting right next to her.

Soccer. Video games. Cute clothes. Lived in a hotel. Omigod. That was no coincidence. A.A. realized the awful truth: Cecily was a total A.A. clone. No wonder Tri was into her. And no wonder Tri was so rude to A.A. these days—he didn't like her anymore, and he didn't need her anymore.

He was over her in every possible way. And that was fine: Of course it was. A.A. had a boyfriend of her own, whose name she couldn't remember right now. But she liked him. A lot. Plus, she had the Ashleys. She didn't need dumb, two-timing, playa-hating Tri Fitzpatrick.

So why did she feel like throwing up?

11

LILI CRACKS OPEN THE DANGEROUS BOOK FOR GIRLS

HOW MUCH STUFF DO YOU NEED FOR ONE night, anyway?"

A.A. stood with her hands on her hips, her pretty face looking puzzled, surveying the small forest of Nordstrom bags growing in the middle of her bedroom. After they'd spent way too much money on clothes, Lili had convinced her to help pick out camping gear for her upcoming trip.

Ashley's mom had ordered her home after her credit-card company called to ask if the Visa had been stolen, since someone had rung up thousands of dollars in charges in less than an hour; and a cranky Dex had picked up Lauren to bring her home and wouldn't take no for an excuse, saying something about having just driven a very long, very circuitous route that had taken all afternoon.

She and Lili had returned to the Fairmont penthouse loaded down with piles of outdoor equipment. Lili crawled from bag to bag on her hands and knees, checking the contents of each against her credit-card receipt. Clearly, A.A. didn't understand how complicated camping was.

"All the sleeping bags have plaid lining," Lili complained, rifling through one of the larger bags. "It's so 'Seattle'!"

"Did you really need to buy that huge a backpack? It's bigger than you." A.A. sat down on the white lacquered trunk and surveyed the booty.

"I know, it's ugly, right?" Lili flicked the pack's black utilitarian straps. Just looking at it made her feel anxious about this camping trip. She was definitely leaving her comfort zone in every possible way. "But Max said to get the biggest one because of the kind of trip we're going on."

"What kind of trip *are* you going on?" A.A. cocked her head to one side and pulled at a pigtail.

Lili sighed. "A *secret* trip." She rocked back on her heels, shooting A.A. a mournful look. "I'm beginning to think it's a stupid idea. Ashley certainly thinks so."

"Of course it's a stupid idea," A.A. told her. "I mean, think about it. You've never been camping before in your life. You've never even *wanted* to go camping. Your mother would go ballistic if she knew what you were up to. The other people going are weirdos from the School of Rock. And the whole reason you're doing it is to impress some boy."

"Not to impress him," Lili argued, though she knew she didn't sound very convincing. "Just so we can . . . you know, hang out."

A.A. made a face. "You can hang out anywhere *in the city*," she pointed out. "You do realize Genghis Khan will *kill* you if she finds out about this," she added, using their private nickname for Lili's hard-liner mom. Lili didn't mind too much—she'd come up with the nickname herself.

"That's why I'm keeping it all." Lili grinned, though she didn't feel much like smiling right now. The thought of her mother finding out . . . it was way too scary to even consider.

"How about when she sees the credit-card bill?"

"My dad is the one who pays my card," said Lili, standing up. All this crawling about was giving her sore legs, and she needed to be in top physical condition for the trip. "He never asks questions. And if he does, I'll tell him it's for Ashley's birthday present. That's why we got all this stuff at Nordstrom rather than some outdoor shop."

"Just admit it. You wouldn't be seen dead in an outdoor shop," A.A. joked, throwing a sheepskin-covered cushion at Lili.

"I don't even know what an outdoor shop is," Lili said. "Or *where* it is. Thank God they even sell this stuff at Nordstrom. Okay, let's go through our plan again for next

Saturday. I'll get dropped off here after my violin lesson. Are you sure your mother is here next weekend?" It was the day before Thanksgiving and everyone would be going away or celebrating over the weekend, so Lili wanted to go over the plan before A.A. got too distracted by turkey and stuffing.

It was crucial that A.A.'s mother be present and accounted for, because there was no way Lili's parents would let her stay over without adult supervision. Even if the adult in question was Jeanine Alioto, a former supermodel who spent half her time traveling and thought being a good mother meant making sure the maid brought in a tray of hot milk and warm cookies every night.

"She said she would be. But you know her." A.A. grinned. "Someone might invite her to the Venice Film Festival or something, and she'll fly off."

"Try and persuade her to stay, okay?" Lili needed everything to go according to plan. Jeanine wouldn't even notice if Lili disappeared almost as soon as she arrived—A.A.'s mother usually spent her Saturday afternoons getting a hot-stone massage and top-down body waxing, in preparation for some glamorous event that night. Then she'd be out all evening and asleep half of Sunday. By then Lili would be safely back in the city and nobody over the age of fourteen would be any the wiser. But Jeanine actually had to be *in the country* for this plan to work.

"So you have your pack and your sleeping bag." A.A. picked up her school skirt, the most despised item in her closet, and lobbed it onto her loft bed. "What else?"

"Hiking boots," said Lili, lifting a pair of tan Timberlands out of their giant box, their thick dark laces tied together. "*So* not flattering. Water bottle. Fleece vest. A flashlight I can wear around my head for nighttime bathroom visits."

"Lil," A.A. said. "You do know that there aren't any bathrooms up on Mount Tam. You know there are just bushes, right?"

"Yeah, of course I do!" Lili protested. She'd been hoping there would be little blocks of bathrooms, like mini log cabins, studded along the walking trails. Why not? If she were chief park ranger, she would have them built. Maybe with cute little skylights to let in the sun, and biodegradable toilet paper, and laminated reading material about local flora and fauna. Places people could recharge their cell phones. Maybe there could be wireless hot spots, so you could even check your e-mail!

"Bushes crawling with snakes and raccoons and spiders," A.A. rattled off, as she lay back on the trunk, attempting to juggle her school shoes.

"Thanks, A.A." Lili sighed. She hoped A.A. was joking. "You're so *supportive*."

"You know what I think. Doing all this for some guy . . . well, it's just not worth it." A.A. seemed very down on guys at the moment. For someone who was going out with her first-ever boyfriend, this was kind of surprising. Wasn't A.A. in love?

Lili wanted to explain how much she liked Max. She wanted to go on the camping trip to show him she was a good sport, and someone who shared in his interests. Plus, she couldn't stand the thought of him being up on the mountain with just his grotty friends and their skanky girlfriends for company.

"Just tell me it's all going to work out next Saturday," Lili begged her. She pulled the fleece vest out of its tissue wrap and held it up to her petite frame. "What do you think?"

A.A. mimed throwing up.

"I know," said Lili. She never thought things would come to this: a burgundy fleece vest and a flashlight strapped to her forehead. Is this what you had to do when you had a boyfriend? She tugged off the vest and crammed it back into the shopping bag. The weather forecast predicted rain and high winds for the weekend. Perhaps the trip would be called off. Perhaps she could return all this horrible stuff and use the store credit for some cute outfits. God knows, she deserved it.

The intercom buzzed and Lili leaped up, feeling instantly guilty. Her mother must be downstairs, parked outside the Fairmont's main lobby, waiting to drive Lili home.

"Have a happy turkey day," Lili said, giving A.A. a hug. "And remind your mother to be here," she whispered, as though her conversation with A.A. was being monitored. "My life depends on it."

A.A. waved her hand as if to say, *Don't worry about it*. But Lili couldn't help worrying. If one small thing went wrong, her perfect plans might crumble. And what would happen then, Lili didn't dare to think about.

12

LAUREN RECEIVES
AN INVITATION TO
CHANGE HER MIND

AUREN STRETCHED OUT HER LEGS AND TRIED
not to yawn. The chairs in the Little Theater were
way uncomfortable. That was the point, she
guessed: Nobody would be able to doze off during MODs
(Middle-of-the-Day announcements). She tapped one
Louboutin Mary Jane on the parquet floor, trying to
drown out the droning voice of Miss Evangelista, the
music teacher, who'd been talking about everyone getting
their forms in for the Glee Club trip to the symphony.
Yawn! Why did the teachers take up so much time during
MODs? Didn't they know that the real business went on
after they'd left the stage?

This Monday, in particular, something big was going
down. The entire seventh grade was buzzing about Ashley

Spencer's party which was two weeks away. Ever since she'd been spotted that morning on the stone bench outside the playground, shuffling party invitations as though they were a deck of Tarot cards, nobody had been able to concentrate for a second on schoolwork.

Lauren found their anxiety catching, even though unlike most of the other girls, she *knew* she was invited to Ashley's party. All the Ashleys had received their invitations at the Fillmore Starbucks that morning, while they were waiting to pick up their venti decaf soy lattes. Ashley's favorite drink.

Finally the teachers were filing off the stage and the other grades were beginning to disperse, headed to class or early lunch. But the seventh graders hung around, giggling and nudging one another, taking way too long to make their way out of the theater.

And there was Ashley, standing smack-bang in the middle of things, like the eye of a hurricane, holding all the cards, so to speak, and acting as if she had no idea why anyone was making such a fuss.

"Melody Myers!" Ashley had started calling out names. Those lucky enough to get an invitation simpered up to her, acting all surprised and honored. "Sheridan Riley!"

The strange thing about the whole scene was that Ashley didn't appear to be enjoying herself all that much. Usually she loved lording it over the rest of the grade, or having her status as the queen of cool dangled in front of other people's noses.

But today she was looking almost overwhelmed, as though she couldn't quite believe *how* big a deal all this was. She didn't even have all the Ashleys there to support her. Lili had managed to wriggle out of class for what she said was a doctor's appointment, but Lauren knew what she was really doing: Lili and Max were meeting up to go shopping for more camping equipment. Apparently he had taken one look at her Nordstrom gear and deemed it all wrong. Max was taking her to a real sports shop.

Lili and Ashley weren't on the best of terms anyway right now, something Lauren was watching with interest. After their velvet-dress showdown in the store on Saturday afternoon, Lili was furious. When Lauren was paying for her clothes, Lili joined her at the counter, whispering that something was up with Ashley's party. At the time, Lauren thought Lili was just suffering from robe rage. But the more she thought about it, the more she thought Lili might be onto something.

Ashley called out another name. "Bethany Revson!"

Lauren hung back by the stack of chairs, watching some girls' faces get longer and longer as they realized they were doomed to be Cinderellas, not going to the ball.

Daria Hart looked like she was about to cry. Even

Guinevere Parker seemed disappointed, though she must have known she would *never* be invited to Ashley's party, not in a million years, no matter how loudly she talked about wanting to write a style report on the party for Miss Gamble's school newspaper. And there was poor Sadie, her nose in the air, pretending not to care.

Sadie was still a little annoyed about being ditched abruptly the other day. "I'm not hanging around here," she told Lauren. "This is stupid. Why does everyone care so much about a dumb party? I'm going to class."

"Okay." Lauren nodded, nervously looking over her shoulder to see if any of the Ashleys noticed her talking to Sadie.

"Why do you keep doing that?" Sadie demanded, glaring at Lauren through her thick glasses.

"What?"

"Looking over your shoulder whenever you talk to me."

Lauren felt a stab of guilt. She hadn't realized she was so transparent.

"Anyway, do you really think you have a shot at getting an invitation? Get real, Lauren!"

Lauren didn't know how to answer that—the force of Sadie's vehemence surprised her. But she didn't have to say anything, since Lili said it for her.

Lili arrived at the Little Theater a bit out of breath.

"Lauren! Do you have your invite? I think I left mine at Starbucks this morning, and I need to tell Max the date of the party."

Lauren rooted in her handbag and handed the precious invitation to Lili, while Sadie looked on with wide eyes. Lili flicked a curious glance in Sadie's direction, then excused herself to finish her phone call with her boyfriend.

Sadie looked at Lauren. "You're invited to Ashley's party."

"Um, sort of." Lauren felt a wrenching guilt. "There's, um, something I've been meaning to tell you."

Sadie's eyes narrowed. "I think I can guess. I was wondering when you would tell me about your 'new friends.' You think I didn't know that you're one of them now? I might not dress as well as they do, but I'm not stupid."

Lauren felt ill.

"I totally saw you at Blowfish Sushi the other day—and saw you running away so you wouldn't have to say hi to me. And the other afternoon, you didn't have to help your mom, right? You were meeting *them*, weren't you?" Sadie nodded as if Lauren's silence confirmed her suspicions.

Sadie smacked her palm on her forehead. "Of course! That's why you keep insisting we sneak off campus for lunch. You don't want to be seen with me at the ref! I'm not good enough to hang out with you anymore!"

"It's not like that," Lauren pleaded, trying to keep her

voice low so nobody else would overhear their conversation. Not that she needed to worry. There was plenty of noise echoing through the half-empty theater, girls squealing with delight over their invitations or whispering worriedly in quiet clusters.

A fight had broken out when Ashley called the name Catherine. Both Catherine Diega and Kathryn Black were convinced they were the rightful recipients, and they managed to rip the envelope in two before A.A. intervened, pulling them apart and telling them they were both invited.

"Whatever," Sadie said scornfully. She looked contemptuously from Lauren to the Ashleys in the center of the throng. To Lauren's horror, Sadie walked right up to Ashley and planted her hands on her hips.

"No one cares about your party," Sadie declared.

"What did you say?" asked Ashley.

"You heard me."

Ashley's cheeks went bright red. She looked Sadie up and down. She turned to A.A. and Lili and laughed. "Who are you?"

Sadie didn't know how to answer.

"Oh, right. You're the girl who had to move all the way to Connecticut because you have no friends here." Ashley was smiling so forcefully it looked like a clown's grin. Her voice was as cold as Antarctica before global warming. "I think you're just saying that because you're not invited. And it's not like anyone's ever going to invite you to any party, ever. Because let's face it, *no one likes you*."

Sadie's cheeks turned scarlet, and her eyes brimmed with tears. Lauren was shocked into silence.

That was really mean of Ashley. Okay, so maybe Sadie was rude, but Ashley was way out of line. People said stuff like that online or in texts all the time, but Ashley had said it out loud, to her face.

Lauren felt awful, then angry. Sadie didn't deserve that. Maybe she was a little bit of a baby and a lot socially backward, but she was a person. She was human. She was still Lauren's friend.

"Wait!" she called. But Sadie had already slammed the Little Theater doors.

Lauren looked around, feeling her anger build. Couldn't Ashley see what she was doing? Didn't she know how mean this was, making the uninvited stand around like losers at a beauty pageant? It wasn't as though Ashley had to have a small party; she could afford to invite the whole school. She just wanted to show everyone how badly she could make them feel.

And eviscerating Sadie was just the worst.

"Okay—that's it!" Ashley handed out the final invitation, and the left-behinds started to drift out of the room, leaning on one another for comfort. Sheridan Riley was talking in an overloud voice about what she planned to wear, oblivious to the dejected expressions of half the girls still in the room.

Ashley herself had the weirdest look on her face. If Lauren didn't know her better, she'd think it was guilt. Or maybe remorse. But this was Ashley Spencer. The closest thing she felt to remorse was when she found something she'd bought at full price on the sale rack.

Then Ashley began giggling with Lili and A.A., and Lauren heard "loser" and "Boogers" in between their laughter. She made up her mind right then: It had to stop. No more exclusive parties! No more crying and feeling like rejects! No more in and out lists!

Lauren felt invigorated by a bright new idea. Who said old and new friends couldn't mix? So what if Ashley had dissed Sadie just now? Ashley had called Lauren a loser for years, and now they were practically BFFs. Since when did Ashley Spencer ever think for herself? Lauren had manipulated her way into the Ashleys, and she was sure she could do the same for Sadie. Working alone wasn't getting Lauren anywhere. But with Sadie as one of the Ashleys, the two of them working on the inside could totally bring the Ashleys down.

Of course, for her new plan to work, Sadie had to get a

makeover. Her clothes and shoes and hairstyle needed a seismic adjustment. She had to get glamorized. Lauren knew that this was possible: Hadn't she done exactly the same thing this summer? Plus, even Lili and A.A. had noticed that without the glasses and in normal clothing, Sadie looked decent.

Sadie had potential. With an outfit or two from Lauren's extensive designer wardrobe, a sharp, chic haircut from an exclusive salon, a pair of color-tinted contact lenses to turn Sadie's brown eyes blue, and some lessons in take-charge attitude, Sadie could rival any of the Ashleys. She could *be* an Ashley.

Any ambivalence Lauren had felt about her secret plan to crush the Ashleys was gone. She felt keen with purpose, and she knew just where to begin. She was going to get Sadie—and the whole seventh grade—invited to Ashley's super-exclusive birthday party.

Lauren knew exactly how to do it. All it would take was rounding up a few of the disgruntled rejects to place some very important phone calls to someone as insecure and power-crazed as Ashley herself—Lili.

13

ASHLEY FACES A JURY
OF HER PEERS?

ASHLEY COULD NOT BELIEVE HER EARS. SHE'D just slid into her chair for Manners & Morals, in front of a formal place setting. They were learning dining etiquette that week. The first course had been served—some sort of cold, slimy appetizer. Was it calamari? No, apparently it was some kind of French-braised octopus. They were supposed to eat using the correct utensils while making polite conversation. But the question she'd just heard was anything but polite.

"What did you say again?"

"I said, is it true you're facing the Honor Board this afternoon?" Guinevere Parker looked like she would faint if Ashley directed another glare in her direction.

"I'm what?" Ashley looked at her friends for backup.

A.A. was too busy poking dubiously at her appetizer to answer, and Lili couldn't meet her eye.

"It's true," Lili finally admitted, picking up her salad fork and looking skeptically at the food on her plate. "I didn't want to bring it up earlier, but, um, here's your summons."

"Excuse me?" Ashley was floored. She looked at the little piece of paper Lili had handed her.

She, Ashley Matilda Diana Spencer (yes she was named after *that* people's princess), had been summoned to appear before Miss Gamble's Honor Board. The Honor Board! Like she was some common criminal, plagiarist, or cheat!

"But aren't you the head of the Honor Board?" Ashley asked, her voice ringing with betrayal as she pushed her plate away in annoyance. She scowled at Lili. "Can't you do something about this?"

Lili shook her head primly. "I'm sorry, but that's not how the board works."

Ashley decided she wouldn't worry. She had appeared before the Honor Board before. It met once a month in the oak-paneled school library, a room with ornate molded ceilings, a huge chandelier, glass-fronted bookshelves, and a giant central table rumored to have come from Thomas Jefferson's house, Monticello.

And once a month, Ashley was called in because she had three late notices. Whatever! Nothing happened. Lili made a solemn little speech, and everyone nodded, and then someone told Ashley how cool her hairstyle was, or asked her where she got her new handbag. She promised to try not to be tardy in future and then swanned off to lunch. A cakewalk.

"Didn't Honor Board already meet for the month?" Ashley asked, finally taking a small bite and grimacing. Miss Charm told them that part of being citizens of the world was developing a sophisticated palette. Last week they'd dined on a selection of raw fish: ceviche, crudo, and sushi.

Lili nodded. "Uh-huh, but this is, um, a special meeting."

Ashley couldn't help but notice that Guinevere was taking it all in. This was so not cool. The Ashleys always put up a united front—if word got out that there was infighting in the ranks, then what were the Ashleys but just another group of girls banded together for fear of being alone?

She wanted to wig out on Lili: Her parents would definitely lose it if they found out . . . she was already on thin ice . . . she'd barely gotten her party back on track—if what her parents were planning could even be *called* a party at this point (Ashley shuddered when she saw the crepe-paper decorations Matilda had picked up at Party City). It was the reason why she hadn't been so gung-ho on going into detail or shopping for outfits. But an Honor Board demerit would sink any party, lame or not.

There could be only one reason she was being called

before the board: It had to be because she was late on Monday, didn't it? There couldn't be something else, could there?

"What did I miss?" Lauren asked, scooting into the empty seat next to A.A. and looking askance at the rubbery mess in front of her. "How am I supposed to eat this exactly?"

"Fish knife!" Ashley explained, holding up the correct silverware. "And I'm surprised you haven't heard. Apparently, it's all over school: I'm being called in front of the Honor Board—but I have no idea why!"

"That sucks," said Lauren, looking nervous all of a sudden. Then she quickly brightened up. "Hey, if you need a student defender, I'll do it."

Normally Ashley didn't bother with a defender, because it was hard to defend a late notice slapped on you by an overzealous, fashion-challenged teacher. Just admit the crime, do the time. Ashley usually got away with a painless "warning."

But this time Ashley agreed to have Lauren argue her case. Everyone knew Lauren was smart. If anyone could outfox Lili and her Honor Board vixens, it would be Lauren Page.

"It'll be okay, I'm sure," Lili soothed, wiping her mouth carefully with a napkin as one of the refectory workers took their plates away and replaced them with bowls full of what their menu said were "sweetbreads," although they looked more like fried brains, which, they were soon not too pleased to learn, was exactly what they were.

"Uh-huh, thanks for nothing, Benedict Arnold Li," Ashley grumbled.

"It's out of my hands, honest," Lili swore, gagging on a particularly chewy piece.

After the last class of the day, Ashley met up with Lauren in front of the library doors.

"Like I told you, I have no idea what this is about," Ashley complained, not bothering to lower her voice. Let the cries of the prisoner echo through the halls of Miss Gamble's!

"Whatever it is, I'm sure we can get you off the hook," Lauren reassured her. "Just promise me you'll stay calm and let me do all the talking. Well, most of it—okay?"

Ashley nodded. Lauren rapped on the heavy door of the library.

"Enter!" That was her friend formerly known as Lili, seated at the head of the giant oak table. Arranged in a U around the table were her myopic-looking Honor Board cronies, Supriya Manapali, Cameron Welch, and Vicky Zimmerman.

Ashley sniffed and held her head high, leading Lauren to the other end of the table. For these girls, Honor Board was as close as they'd ever come to knowing power—whereas

Ashley knew it every day. She pitied them. Really, she did.

"I'm sorry we had to call you in here today," said Lili, and she certainly looked sorry. Just as well. She was on very shaky ground. "But an urgent matter was brought to our attention, and we felt it necessary to address the issue immediately."

"Who's been bitching about me?" Ashley burst out. Lauren placed a calming hand on her arm and shot Ashley a "you promised to be good" look.

"What my client—I mean, Ashley—is asking is this: What is the nature of this urgent matter? Of what is she accused?" Lauren sounded very professional. She probably watched too many *Law & Order* reruns.

"Nobody's accusing anyone," squeaked Supriya.

"The thing is," explained Lili, clicking her Mont Blanc pen and giving Ashley her most earnest look. "I got a lot of calls yesterday concerning what happened during MODs. Some of the girls felt very excluded when you handed out party invitations in public and left some students out. They've gone to the headmistress about it. We had no choice but to call this meeting."

Lauren coughed and kept her eyes on the notebook in front of her.

"According to the complaint," said Cameron, who was only on the Honor Board because her parents had paid for new sectional sofas, a flat-screen TV, and a wet bar for the staff's break room, "you were promoting *clique culture.*"

This was so ridiculous! *Of course* she had to exclude a lot of people from the party—that was the whole point! Some people were just more special than others. Although to be honest, the uninvited wouldn't be missing much. Her party was so downsized, Ashley wouldn't be surprised if her mother showed up with one of those ready-made cakes from Carvel where they spelled out your name in icing right before they rang you up at the checkout.

She had been so sure that by this time Cirque du Ashley would be back on the party-planning menu, but so far nothing had worked. Not crying, not sulking, not locking herself in her room, not threatening to leave home. ("Where would you go? Vermont? Say hi to Aunt Agnes for me!" her mom had said too cheerfully.) Going on a hunger strike didn't make much of an impact. Especially since after two hours Ashley caved in and devoured a whole bag of Pirate's Booty.

The most infuriating thing was, her parents hardly seemed to notice how upset she was. They were completely distracted, as though her party was the last thing on their minds. She had only two more weeks to wear them down.

Otherwise, no one would have any fun at all.

But try telling that to the Honor Board. Besides, Ashley couldn't confess her party was nothing special. It would totally defeat her image.

"Miss Gamble's is founded on the ideals of loyalty, kind-ness, and service to fellow man," Vicky intoned in a solemn voice. "Any deviation of student conduct from school policy can result in a suspension."

Ashley went pale.

Lili looked at her with a "don't kill me" face.

"Suspend me?" Ashley thought she must have misheard. Ashley Spencer, suspended? *That could not happen.* There was no way she could talk her parents into reinstating her party to its former glory if she got suspended!

"Surely there's a simpler solution." Lauren's voice was calm and clear. "Is the problem that Ashley's having a birth-day party?"

"No," Lili conceded. "Of course not. It's that the invita-tions were issued in public, and that some members of the seventh grade were excluded."

"Ashley," said Lauren, fixing her with a serious stare. "How many seventh graders have you invited to your party?"

"I don't know—maybe fifteen?"

"So how many seventh graders do not have invitations?"

"Just the lame ones. Eighteen?"

"What would you say," Lauren said slowly, "to inviting the whole class? That way, nobody would have any reason to complain. They could all come to the party."

Ashley opened her mouth and closed it again. Invite

everyone to her house? Let the plebes in to gaze at the imperial family? How very déclassé.

"I mean," Lauren continued, staring at her hard, "you have enough space, right? And I believe that solution would be acceptable to the board, yes?"

All the board members nodded enthusiastically. Especially since none of them had been issued invitations. They reminded Ashley of the three wise monkeys, except monkeys were cuter.

Lili gave Ashley a long look of her own, as if to say, *This is your chance.*

Ashley sighed. She knew when the cards were stacked against her. "Oh, all right," she said. "Why not?"

Lauren's face cracked into a broad smile, her eyes sparkling in triumph. "So the board agrees—no suspension?" she asked quickly.

"No suspension!" they chorused, Lili's voice the loudest of all. Supriya and Cameron giggled with relief, and even Vicky, who usually only smiled when something bad happened to someone else, looked supremely self-satisfied.

What a pack of sheep! Or was that flock of sheep? Whatever! Ashley had outwitted them—with Lauren's help, of course. Sure she had to invite a freak show to her party, but hello: It did have a circus theme, right?

The main thing was—no suspension. Plus, now she had

the perfect argument to present to her parents. *Mom, Dad, I would have just loved to have a small close-friends-only event like you were planning, but . . . Miss Gamble's won't let me!*

She *had* to have her big party now. Ha! Ashley knew her mom would cave when she told her that Miss Gamble's school policy practically called for an insane blowout. Everything was working out perfectly.

Ashley beamed back at the Honor Board geeks as she followed a triumphant Lauren out of the room.

They wanted to attend a party? She was going to throw the biggest, baddest, and hands-down-no-jokes-about-it-this-one-is-for-the-record-books-*best* party anyone had ever seen.

Send in the clowns, jugglers, sword swallowers, lion tamers, acrobats, and contortionists! The tower of pink and white cupcakes, the fifty-foot tent, the celebrity guests, the razzle and the dazzle.

Ashley Spencer was turning thirteen!

14

THE PERILS OF BEING
A TOMBOY

ASHLEY INVITED HER FRIENDS TO SIT IN on a meeting with Mona Mazur the next day. Lili and A.A. were charmed, intimidated, and appalled by Mona's grandiose plans and haughty personality. Only Lauren hadn't been able to join them, because she had some sort of hair appointment. A.A. didn't know anyone who scheduled a haircut as often as Lauren did. Not even her mother went to Étienne Étoile (née Stephen Star, hair god to the stars) every two weeks!

During the brainstorming session with Mona, A.A. noticed that Ashley didn't appear at all fazed by the fact that the Honor Board had ordered her to invite the whole seventh-grade class to the party. Ashley usually didn't take too kindly to other people telling her what to do, but she didn't seem to mind at all this time.

As for never wanting to talk about her party before, now it seemed the party was all Ashley ever wanted to talk about. She hogged all conversations to regale them with details on how a famous French act was going to high-dive into the pool, and how they had to convince the staff to volunteer to be shot out from the cannon. News of her party had even reached the former producers of *Preteen Queen*, who were interested in taping it for their new show on the Sugar cable network, *Spoiled Rotten*.

The whole thing made A.A.'s head swim. She was glad to be home finally and away from all the hype. She found Ned and his friends hanging out in the vast open-plan living room. Ned wasn't bad at all, as brothers went. Or so A.A. thought—none of the other Ashleys had a brother. If you had to have a brother, she decided, they should be like Ned: slightly older, smart, and easygoing.

The only problem with Ned was his choice of friends.

Usually A.A. didn't care who was clustered around the giant flat-screen TV, brandishing a joystick and screeching every time an alien life form or king of the underworld exploded and/or bit the dust. But today she minded. She minded a whole lot.

"No way!" Tri was shouting at the screen, trying to drown out the jeers of the other guys.

"He's got you, man." Ned was laughing.

A.A. dropped onto the raspberry chenille sofa, the latest

addition to the living room. Her mother was under the influence of a new designer, who insisted that fruit colors in a room were the equivalent of supplements in a smoothie, i.e., vital to your physical and mental health. Only her mother would buy an idea like that, A.A. thought—but then, her mother was always open to ideas that involved spending wads of her alimony payments on clothes, shoes, or home decor.

"Foiled again, Fitzpatrick," cackled the guy sprawled on the floor—he had dark hair and frameless glasses and was even taller than Ned. His name was something weird, A.A. remembered—like Ziggy or something. Ned's real name was Zed Starlight, the result of having Jeanine for a mother and an aging British rock star for a father, but he'd traded that in for a more normal name years ago. Ziggy, however, seemed to revel in it.

Next to lanky Ned, long-legged Ziggy (real name Sigmund), and model-tall A.A., Tri was pretty much a midget. A.A. felt wickedly glad of this. She wanted him to feel small in every way today. She was in no mood for his snide jibes.

"I'll play," she announced, reaching for the spare controller that was now kept in a woven banana-skin basket by the fireplace and wriggling to the edge of the sofa. "That is, if you're out, Tri."

"Oh, he's out all right," shouted Ziggy. He propped

himself up on bony elbows, not even bothering to look around at A.A.—Ned's friends were used to her hanging out. The only time they got annoyed with her was when she nabbed the last slice of pizza.

Tri scowled at her, climbing up off the Tibetan rug and stomping over to the other end of the raspberry sofa. A.A. decided to tune him out. He was probably going to try and throw her off her game.

"Go!" Ziggy called to her, and A.A. focused on the screen. Her character, Kandace Kick-Butt, had to leap over a ravine, scale a cliff, and do a backflip over a slobbering tiger in order to make it to the next level. Leaning and twisting her way across the dangerous landscape, it was all A.A. could do to stay upright on the sofa.

"Watch your back!" Ned shouted, throwing a cushion at her, and for a second A.A. was confused, thinking he meant *her* back rather than Kandace's. She swung her head around and saw nothing, of course, but the high nubbly rim of the sofa and the window where Ned had drawn the raw-silk curtains to keep light from reflecting off the screen.

"What the . . . !" Ziggy was back in the game now, his character Adam Avarice springing back into action on screen. "I saved you this time, dude, but I can't do this alone."

"Sorry!" A.A. fixed her gaze on the screen again, but not

117

before glimpsing a smirk on Tri's face. She was determined to show him how much better she was at this game than he was—how much better she was at *everything* than he was. Together with Zig/Adam, she made it to the next canyon, and on to the next round of adversaries. But while her male counterpart was busy leapfrogging a knife-edged cactus, A.A. couldn't help glancing at Tri again.

"What are you looking at?" he snapped, as she looked at the face that she used to think was cute once upon a time. "No wonder you keep messing up."

"Are you serious?" A.A. turned her eyes to the screen. Kandace had a tricky splits-over-a-crevasse maneuver to perform if Adam was going to escape the piranha-infested river with his lycra trousers intact. There! She'd nailed it. "You're the one who's so vain. Thinking everything is about you!"

"Why don't you go find some girls to hang out with?" he sneered, poking her in the back with one foot.

"Don't touch me!" she hissed, twisting away.

"Coming at you, A.A.!" Ned warned her, his mouth half-full of cookies. Jeanine would kill him if she found chocolate chip pieces on the cream-colored armchair, but he was probably counting on Jeanine being distracted right now: She had a new boyfriend in Santa Barbara, some film direc-tor who owned a winery, and spent most of her time zipping up and down the Pacific coast in his private jet, trying to persuade him to redecorate its interior in blueberry and melon ("colors soothing to the sky").

"Oh crap!" Onscreen, Kandace took a hard blow from a tumbling boulder, leaving Adam to clamber on alone. "Look what you made me do!"

Tri said nothing. Ned had stuffed the rest of the cookies in his mouth and grabbed a joystick: He and Ziggy/Adam were soon soaring up the side of a cliff. A.A. tossed her controller onto the floor and sat back on the sofa, turning her head to glower at Tri. He was such a pill. She didn't understand why Ned let him hang out so often. Who needed a grumpy dwarf spoiling everything? They may as well just buy a garden gnome and stand it in front of the fireplace. At least it wouldn't talk. It certainly wouldn't eat all the pizza.

"Where's Hunter tonight?" Tri glared straight back at her. "Don't tell me he's sick of you already?"

"None of your business," she retorted. It was weak, but she was too mad to think of anything smart to say. Actually, she didn't know what Hunter was up to right now, and she didn't really care. They were still going out, officially, but he didn't text her fifty times a day anymore, and when he did try to reach her, she often just blew him off.

He was nice and all, and he still liked her, as far as she

knew. But it was hardly the romance of the century. Maybe love and stuff just wasn't going to work out for her. After she kissed Tri at the Seven party, all it did was drive him back into the arms of Ashley anyhow.

"I did warn you about him. Maybe he's just playing you," Tri suggested, his voice low. A.A. could barely speak. How could she ever have liked Tri? She really hated his guts now. His new girlfriend was welcome to him. Actually, A.A. felt sorry for her—she probably had no idea what a dweeb she was dating.

"You total jackass," she hissed back. "*You're* the player! You totally played me."

Tri looked floored. "What are you talking about?"

"As if you don't know!" She folded her arms, pretending to be interested in the video game still going on, but her eyes couldn't focus. "You say you're about to break up with Ashley, but that was just one big lie. Next thing I know, you're Velcro'd to her side. That's the last time I believe a *word* you say."

"Look, I . . . you have to know what really happened." Tri sat forward, his face crumpling and his voice suddenly hoarse. "It's not what you think."

"I don't *think* anything," A.A. shot back. Her phone, slung onto the coffee table when she sat down, started trilling and vibrating at the same time. "I *know*. End of discussion."

"Man, your phone's loud," complained Ziggy, writhing on the floor.

"Okay, okay." A.A. grabbed it and peered at the screen. It was Ashley. Another person she didn't really feel like speaking to right now. The phone stopped ringing, and then almost immediately started trilling again. Whatever Ashley had to say, it was obviously urgent.

Without a backward glance at Tri, A.A. marched off to her bedroom to answer the phone and find out what was so earth-shatteringly important.

15

MISSION: MAKEOVER, OR
MISSION: IMPOSSIBLE?

IS THIS REALLY NECESSARY?" SADIE LOOKED UP at
Lauren from underneath several layers of tinfoil. The
smell of hair dye permeated Lauren's bathroom,
which had been turned for the day into a full-scale replica
of a beauty salon.

Lauren had prescribed major high- and low-lights all
over. Platinum on top, honey blond on the bottom, and fat,
juicy, buttery streaks everywhere. But for now, Sadie looked
like nothing more than a tinsel Christmas tree.

After the showdown at MODs the other day, it had taken
all of Lauren's charm to win Sadie's trust back. Still, even
though she was still a little peeved, Sadie was a realist.
Without Lauren, she had nobody. Plus, she seemed to
accept the fact that Lauren was one of the Ashleys now, as
long as Lauren made time for her as well.

Once they'd patched things up over a tedious game of Sorry!, Lauren had gently suggested that Sadie might want to change the way she looked and acted if she wanted to have a better life at Miss Gamble's, and offered all the resources at her disposal, including her hairstylist, personal shopper, and life coach.

If only Sadie would be more appreciative! It had been hell trying to book an at-home visit with Étienne, who was based in New York. Her mother had told her he'd had to bump Maria Shriver and Hayden "Pantywear" to squeeze Lauren in. What Trudy hadn't known was that the appointment was really for Sadie.

"Trust me," Lauren said, leaning on the marble counter. "Or really, trust Étienne."

Sadie sighed so forcefully she rattled several of the tinfoil squares. "Tsk tsk!" Étienne scolded, continuing to brush, wrap, and fold.

Lauren was glad when her phone began to buzz, offering some relief from Sadie's constant agonizing over what Étienne was doing to her hair. You'd think she was getting a root canal instead of a beauty treatment.

Lauren left the room and pulled out her phone. It was a text from Christian. Of her two boyfriends, Christian was probably her favorite. He was so funny and goofy, his dark blond hair always adorably disheveled, his green eyes sparkling at her. She read his message.

R U HOME?

JUST, she texted back.

COOL. ON MY WAY.

What? Lauren was startled. They hadn't arranged to meet up today. She thought Christian had crew practice on Wednesday afternoons. In fact, she *knew* he had practice, because her other boyfriend—dark, brooding Alex—was on the crew team at Saint Aloysius and had practice on Thursdays, and Lauren had to be very careful about scheduling her dates with them accordingly. Practice must have been canceled.

SURE, C U SOON, she texted, but there was no reply. She dropped her phone onto the glass-topped vanity.

"What do you think?" asked Sadie, as Étienne unwrapped one square of tinfoil to show Lauren the developing color.

"Nice," said Lauren, as her phone buzzed again. Maybe Christian was here already and wanted her to come outside. Her mother intimidated him, and Lauren thought he might be annoyed by Trudy's occasional habit of calling him "Chrissy." She picked up her phone and checked the message, trying to disregard Sadie's pout.

R U AROUND?

Oh no.

It was Alex.

2 L8—GOING OUT, she texted back frantically. The last

thing she needed was Alex dropping by while Christian was here. This house was big, but not big enough for two boyfriends wanting her undivided attention. Her mother knew what was going on and was even secretly proud.

Sadie would probably think she was kind of slutty, trying to have two relationships at once. Maybe she was kind of slutty. But there wasn't time to worry about that now!

DEX SEZ UR HERE.

Yikes! Lauren felt her face sizzling. Alex was obviously outside in the driveway, chatting with Dex. Didn't Dex have work to do? Computer work that involved being inside? He'd probably let Alex in the gate and blabbed that she was in there, hanging out with a friend. Christian was going to be here any minute. What was she going to do?

"Lauren!" Her mother's singsong voice rang out on the intercom, a recent addition to her room. Trudy said she was tired of sending text messages to Lauren every time she wanted to tell her something, so now they had a bothersome intercom system. "Christian's at the door, honey."

"Coming," she croaked. This was the worst possible news. How was she going to get out of this disaster?

"Who's Christian?" asked Sadie, looking up from her magazine. Lauren's head was spinning too fast to answer the question.

"Just stay here—I won't be long," she mumbled, racing

out of her room and along the hallway. She had to get there as quickly as possible, to drag Christian out of sight before Alex arrived. But hang on—wasn't Alex already there, chewing the fat with Dex in the driveway? Lauren's Olympic-speed slowed to a crawl. There wasn't any point in rushing if all she was rushing into was a whole heap of trouble.

Trudy was hovering in the glass-fronted front lobby; Lauren could see her from the end of the second hallway. Her mother looked bemused and excited, the way she always did when Christian or Alex came over, as though she was delighted to have a daughter who was so popular and grown-up all of a sudden. *Too* popular, thought Lauren glumly, dragging herself the final few feet toward the lobby. Trudy's mouth opened and closed; she stared at Lauren and shook her head. What?

Lauren rounded the corner, her heart thudding, into the sun-filled, marble-floored lobby. And there they were.

Christian. And Alex. Chatting. *Laughing.*

"I'll get chef to bring out some lemonade," Trudy decided, flapping off in the direction of the kitchen. For a split second Lauren thought about grabbing her, begging her to stay. But it was too late. Her mother had gone, and she was alone with her boyfriends. Make that ex-boyfriends. The two of them had figured it out, right?

But what was so funny?

"Hey, there you are," Christian drawled. "What's up?"

"I just came over to drop off your Latin book—you left it the other day," Alex said, handing over the thick textbook. "Thanks for all the help. I'd stay, but my mom's already annoyed I'm not home in time for her paella. See you, Chris. Later, Lauren." Then he disappeared into the backseat of his parents' Mercedes and drove away.

"I didn't know you knew Alex," Christian said.

"Yeah . . . we, uh . . . I tutor him in Latin." Lauren shrugged. "How do you know him?" she asked, as her phone started to ring with the thudding beat of 50 Cent's "In Da Club," Ashley's favored ringtone for her birthday-party countdown. Whatever Ashley wanted, it could wait. Lauren forwarded it to voice mail.

"We play in the same lacrosse league," said Christian. "But his team sucks." He grinned.

Lauren nodded. Of course it would make sense that the two of them would know each other. She would have to tread carefully, but it seemed as if her nightmare scenario had not come to pass. They didn't know! They hadn't figured it out! Had she really gotten away with it this time? It appeared so.

"Do you want to come in?"

Christian shook his head. "Nah, I was just in the area and thought I'd say hi." He ruffled her hair. "You look cute in your uniform. But I should go. My dad gets mad when I miss his night with us. Anyway, shouldn't you get that?" he asked, meaning her phone, which had begun to ring again. *It's your birthday, we gon' party . . .* She hit ignore again and sentenced the call to voice mail.

"Bye." Lauren nodded, smiling and stepping into his arms. "You look cute too." She gave Christian a quick kiss, since she could hear Dex out in the graveled driveway, calling to them and laughing. She was going to get teased so badly on the way to school tomorrow. She'd rather catch a bus than listen to one of Dex's lectures about her dental work again.

She waved Christian away as he walked down the hill, feeling more relieved than anything.

"Who was that guy out there?" Sadie asked, when Lauren returned to her bedroom. Étienne was wielding a hair dryer, making final adjustments and fluffing up his masterpiece. Lauren was impressed. Sadie looked like she could be on the cover of a magazine. At least, her hair did.

"What guy?" asked Lauren.

"The dark-haired one? He's a total hottie."

"Oh, that's Alex," Lauren told her, as her phone began to ring again, but Fi'ty didn't sing this time. She held her breath to see if it was Alex, wondering what on earth Christian was doing at her house, or Christian, calling to say he had figured it out and was breaking up with her. But it was just Ashley again. Calling from her home line this time.

Sadie looked in the mirror and studied her new look. "Is he your boyfriend?"

Lauren nodded, not bothering to explain the two-guys scenario. "Can you excuse me?" she told Sadie, taking the phone into the other room. She had to take the call. Even though Lauren was plotting the end of her reign, Ashley Spencer was still not someone she could afford to brush off for very long.

16

THE SCREAM HEARD AROUND
THE WORLD

ASHLEY HAD NEWS, AND WHEN ASHLEY HAD news it could not wait. It required an all-Ashleys conference call, run from the nerve center of the entire operation—her four-poster bed. She'd already wasted ten minutes trying to track everyone down, because apparently everyone was too busy with their own unimportant little lives to help Ashley in her hour of need.

Lili was annoyed because she was about to meet Max to go over last-minute details about their camping trip, A.A. was at home playing video games, and Lauren had yet to pick up the phone—Ashley had spotted her leaving school with Sadie Graham, of all people, but she was too upset right then to deal with that information, because this was a true emergency.

In fact, this was the worst crisis in her entire almost thirteen years of life—much worse than the cancellation of *Preteen Queen*, and much worse than getting dumped by Tri. The first she could pretend she didn't care about, and the second she could lie about. But not this!

This was going to go public. There was *no way* this could be covered up. Ashley flung herself on the bed, speed-dialing each number over and over. The Ashleys had to be the first to know.

"What is it?" Lili demanded. "Max just told me not to forget to buy something called 'deet.' Does anyone even know what that is?"

"It's bug spray. Anyway, Ash, if this is about your party, can it wait until tomorrow?" A.A. moaned. "I'm kind of not in the mood."

"Hello?" Lauren had picked up finally! "What's up? Make it fast, because Étienne gets annoyed when I answer the phone—"

"WILL YOU ALL PLEASE LISTEN!" Ashley shrieked. It was always me, me, me with these girls. "I have some *terrible* news."

"The party's off?" Lili asked, shocked.

"No!"

"You can't get the StripHall Queens? Bummer." That was A.A., of course.

"No!"

"Your parents won't let you invite the whole grade?" asked Lauren. "Maybe I could come talk to them and explain how—"

"BE QUIET!" Ashley roared. "It's not about the party, okay? It's about me. Me and my parents!"

"They're getting *divorced!*" cried Lili, and then there was a clunk like she'd dropped the phone.

"They are so not getting divorced, thank you very much!" Ashley was indignant.

"But your dad's left? Is that it?" A.A. sounded distracted. "Don't worry about it. My dad left, and it's more fun. Plus, he feels so guilty he buys the best Christmas presents. And sometimes Ned's dad sends us random things out of the blue, like that guitar signed by all the members of Linkin Park. Although sometimes the presents aren't that great, like one time he sent us an Ab Roller and we had to give it to the maid."

"Daddy isn't going *anywhere,*" Ashley fumed. "Would you please all stop talking and listen?"

"Sorry, Ashley," said Lauren. That was more like it. Ashley sat up on the bed, legs crossed, phone gripped in trembling fingers.

"My mother," she began, not sure she had the strength to go on. She swallowed. "My mother . . ."

"Has cancer?"

"Is having an affair?"

"Isn't your real mother?"

"MY MOTHER IS PREGNANT!" Ashley shrieked. There was total silence from the other Ashleys. At last, some respect! "My parents just told me. They're all ecstatic about it. They think it's the greatest thing ever!"

"Well," said Lauren slowly, "it could be worse."

"My little sisters are really cute," Lili chimed in. "They let me dress them up like dolls. And your parents'll get a nanny, so it's not like you'll have to clean up after them."

"Are you even listening?" This was not the sympathy Ashley was expecting. Her friends weren't focusing on the key issue: What would people say when they heard this embarrassing news? Wasn't her mother way too old?

This new baby meant that her life as she knew it was essentially over. Ashley loved being an only child. *Loved* it. If—when—her mother had another child, how could she still get all the adoration, affection, and attention she was used to? How would her mother have any energy left to focus on Ashley's needs—her clothes, her social life, her birthday parties—when there was a crying baby in the house?

"Is your party still on?" Lauren seemed anxious.

"It better be," muttered Ashley, pulling a down-filled pillow over her face. She'd only just managed to get her party reinstated to its grand heights of fabulosity after her parents saw the new guest list, and Ashley told them it had to be huge because Miss Gamble's practically dictated it. Her parents better not even think of trying cancellation *part deux*. This baby was already wreaking havoc on her life!

17

THE GIRL WHO CRIED BEAR

ILI LAY ON THE COLD, HARD GROUND LISTENING to the rain pattering on the tent and—even worse— listening to Jezebel and Cassandra giggling about a trick they were planning to play on the boys in the morning. She wasn't really paying attention, but apparently it involved slopping mud into their boots. *Real* mature. If this was camping heaven, then Lili would rather be in hell.

Up on Mount Tam, rain had been falling for most of the afternoon, pretty much ever since Cassandra's dad dropped them off in the public parking lot, telling them to be sure to find a dry spot to pitch their tents. Good advice!

There was no way *her* father would have just dumped them there and driven off. Even though Lili's parents were strict and overprotective, at least they actually cared about their children's welfare. Whereas Cassandra's dad just seemed like he was in a hurry to get back to his pottery wheel or whatever it was he did in his "crafted art" studio.

They'd hiked for two hours to get to the campsite near the river, stumbling over rocks and surrounded by swirling mist. Max had spent more time talking to Jason and Quentin than paying attention to Lili, even when she was almost bent double under the weight of her heavy pack.

It reminded her of the documentary her mother had made her watch about the Long March through China, though at least her feet weren't bound—just crammed into ugly boots. The only thing that cheered her up was seeing Cassandra with mascara streaked down her ghostly pale face.

There wasn't much to feel cheerful about as darkness descended. Their remote campsite wasn't picturesque in any way. Even the river was ugly—wide and muddy, swollen with rain. It was nearly winter, hello! Whose idea was it to go camping now? She had to bunk with the two other girls in a tiny tent, after a disgusting meal of uncooked baked beans, straight from the can, and some soggy slices of bread, eaten standing up.

"Sorry it's too wet to get a fire going," Max apologized, looking cute with his hair wet from the rain.

"It's okay," Lili assured him, knowing Cassandra and Jezebel were more than happy to suffer if it meant Lili was suffering too. Suffering *more*, in fact, because she wasn't used to this. How was this supposed to be fun, exactly?

There were so many other bad things about camping, and as Lili lay in her sleeping bag, pretending to be asleep so she wouldn't have to join in their withering conversation about kids at Reed Prep—or Whiner Junior High, as she liked to think of it—Lili counted them in her mind.

One, Max was too busy doing things—pitching tents, opening cans, finding wood for the damp squib of a fire—to spend any precious alone time with her. Two, when he did draw her into the conversation, it was a disaster: He told them all about Ashley's party, and Lili was forced to invite them all or risk looking like a big snob. Ashley would kill her when she found out that some grungy pseudo-bohos were going to make her party look like a bad episode of *Gossip Girl*.

Number three: She couldn't get a signal on her BlackBerry, so if her mother sent her a message about something—thinking she was safely at A.A.'s, of course, watching a Reese Witherspoon movie marathon—Lili would have no way of either knowing or responding. She was totally cut off from civilization!

By far the very worst thing was having to pee in the bushes. In the rain. In the dark. *Ew!* The whole time, Lili was convinced that either a raccoon was going to leap on her, or she'd fall over with her pants around her ankles (*so* undignified) and end up writhing in the mud.

Okay, so maybe once Max got all that he-man camping stuff out of his system, he had been kind of nice. He had led her away from the others to a small clearing where they could sit on a log and look out over the mountains to watch the sunset.

"I'm so glad you came," he murmured, pulling her close.

"Me too." Lili nestled into the crook of his neck. She gazed dreamily at the russet colors of the setting sun, snuggling deeper as Max put his arms around her.

When he kissed her, it made the treacherous hike in painful, new, too-tight boots almost worth it.

Too soon, it was time to say good night and head on to the girls' bunk, where Jezebel and Cassandra completely ignored her. Let them. Lili was too tired to care. Although when the two girls stopped their incessant whispering and finally drifted off to sleep, Lili was irritated by their loud breathing and occasional piglike snorts.

This was the complete opposite of an Ashleys sleepover. She missed her friends more than anything. If she was there with the Ashleys, they would have sent up SOS signals by now, a rescue helicopter would be on its way, and Ashley's father would be suing the National Park Service.

Lili was too wired to sleep. What was that rustling outside the tent? Maybe it was Max, venturing out in the rain to give her another good-night kiss. How sweet! Lili wriggled out of her sleeping bag and crawled to the zip-fastened opening, taking care not to wake the Scissor Sisters. Slowly, trying to be quiet, she unzipped the entry flap, raindrops pelting her face. She hoped her hair looked okay and stuck her head out.

But it wasn't Max out there in the rainy gloom.

It was a bear.

A huge grizzly that looked just as spooked as Lili.

"AHHHHHHHHHHH!" Lili's scream ripped through camp, waking everyone up. The girls screamed at her to be quiet, while the boys came stumbling out of their tent, boots unlaced, swinging flashlights and cursing under their breath.

"A BEAR! THERE WAS A BEAR!" she yelled.

"You crazy b—," Cassandra was shrieking. "What are you doing sticking your head out of the tent in the middle of the night?"

"Oh my God! You scared us all to death!" cried Jezebel, punching Lili in the shoulder. "Just go back to sleep, loser! There's no bear."

"Lili, it's kind of late in the year for bears," Max told her, crouching down by the tent flap, his fair hair dripping with rain, his voice kind and gentle. "And they don't come down this low, usually. Maybe it was just the shadow of a branch or something."

"Nothing," shouted Jason, who was pacing around the

camp with Quentin, both boys shining their flashlights at the bushes. Both of them looked extremely annoyed to be out in the rain in the middle of the night. "No tracks, either."

"They've probably washed away by now." Lili wanted to cry. She wanted Max to believe her. She knew what she saw!

"Just try and go back to sleep, okay?" He smiled, giving her a quick arm squeeze, and turned off his flashlight. There was nothing Lili could do except climb back into her sleeping bag and try to dismiss the snickering from the other girls. If the bear came back, Lili would make sure it ate those two first.

When she woke up in the morning, after what felt like about two hours of sleep, things were even worse. Lili was bursting to pee, so she pulled on her boots and jacket and upzipped the tent flap.

Oh no!

They must have camped too near the river. She stepped out of the tent and into two inches of muddy water, nearly slipping onto her butt. As far as she could see was a shallow, muddy sea. She sloshed through it to the nearest bushes, wishing she was a million miles from here. Somewhere like a desert. Even the North Pole! Anywhere where it wasn't raining, flooded, and miserable.

Before she made it back to the tent, the boys were up—but they seemed to think the whole thing was really funny. They were skidding through the water, kicking up arcs of muddy slush with their boots and chasing one another around the tents. When Jezebel and Cassandra emerged, rubbing their eyes and talking in loud, sarcastic voices about going bear hunting, they didn't seem unhappy at all.

"Cool—the river's rising!" said Cassandra, scratching at her dyed-red bangs. "Maybe we'll get stranded here—we'll have to miss school tomorrow!"

Lili started to panic.

"We won't get stranded, will we?" she asked Max. "I really need to get back to the city by noon, like you agreed. My mother's coming to the Fairmont to pick me up."

"What's the big hurry?" asked Jezebel, stretching, apparently unconcerned by the drizzle or the huge splotches of mud kicked onto her p.j. bottoms.

"Don't worry," Max reassured her. "If we set off soon, we can make it down to the parking lot in under two hours. Jezebel's father will be waiting for us, and when we're back in the city we'll drop you off first."

"Say what?" yawned Jezebel.

"Your father's picking us up, right?"

"I thought Quentin's father was coming."

"No way," protested Quentin. "We agreed, remember? You were going to ask your dad to come get us."

"Yeah," said Cassandra, giggling, as though something was really funny. "Remember, Jez?"

Jezebel slapped a hand to her forehead. "I guess I forgot to ask him. Oh well! We can just call him and tell him to come. Unless he's doing something else."

"But we can't get phone signals up here," Lili pointed out. Her heart was beating a mile a minute. If they couldn't get a signal until they were down in the parking lot, then that would mean waiting for more than an hour to get picked up.

"Lili's right," said Jason, looking from Quentin to Max. "And I don't even know they'll work there. We'll have to walk down to the lower parking lot, which is much farther. We can probably get there by noon."

"I can call my dad." Max glanced anxiously at Lili. "He'll come right away."

But noon was too late! Lili wanted to scream with frustration. By then, her mother would be waiting for her outside the Fairmont—and, more to the point, discovering that she was not upstairs in A.A.'s penthouse apartment.

By the time they got there, Nancy was sure to be in some furious, tight-lipped rage. Thinking about it made Lili shiver even more in her wet clothes. When Max's father dropped her off, Nancy would see Lili in her muddy, bedraggled outdoor gear, dragging out her pack and sleeping bag and saying good-bye to a group of kids her parents had never met before.

Nancy was a very intelligent woman; she would work

everything out in a flash about the overnight camping trip. She'd know that Lili had lied to her. She'd see the boys in the car. Lili's life would be over.

No doubt about it. If her mother was Genghis Khan, Lili was about to be sent back to China in a body bag.

18

IS THERE SUCH A THING AS
A MODEL MOM?

A.A. HAD SPENT HALF OF SUNDAY MORNING in a state of near panic, wondering when Lili was getting back and obsessing over why she hadn't been in touch. She *knew* this stupid camping trip was a bad idea. Maybe all the rain last night had missed Mount Tam, but somehow A.A. doubted it.

It didn't take long to realize that the whole brilliant plan was in ashes. At noon Lili's mother had arrived at the apartment and been sent away—grim-faced and furious—by a bemused, apologetic Jeanine.

Finally Lili sent a text with the bad news: The trip had been a disaster, she'd missed her ride back to the city, and she'd gotten in touch with her mom, who was about to pick her up at Max's house in St. Francis Wood. Poor Lili!

Ashley's party was less than a week away. What if she wasn't allowed to come? Ashley would never forgive her, and that was a fate worse than death. Worse even than the rage of Lili's parents, maybe. To make things worse, Jeanine was now mad at A.A., as if she were the one who'd lied and snuck off to go camping with boys!

"Don't even think of pulling a stunt like that," her mother told her, pausing mid-dial; she wanted the hotel kitchen to send up a vat of natural yogurt for an at-home spa treatment she was planning that afternoon. "Or I'll send you to live with your miserable father. And you'll never see me or Ned or a video game ever again, because your father is so cheap he's practically free. I swear, you girls! You're barely in your teens, and you're already running away from home."

"Ashley's almost a teenager, and Lili's thirteen already," A.A. couldn't help pointing out. She was standing at the kitchen counter slicing cucumbers for her mother's face mask, trying to make herself useful and prove she was a good, obedient girl, unlike Lili. "It's her party next week, remember?"

"Yeah, well, after the lies you and Lili have been telling us, I don't know if you should go," Jeanine said, screwing up her beautiful face—she could never get the room service number right. Half the time she dialed the gym or the gift store by mistake, and once she even dialed a guest in the hotel.

It wouldn't have been so bad, but she started flirting with

him, and he ended up asking her out to dinner. They dated for a few months. After that, Ned usually did the food ordering. He told A.A. that if they didn't want another stepfather any time soon, they needed to keep Jeanine away from the hotel guests.

"Mom! Don't even joke! You have to let me go!" A.A. nearly sliced off the end of a fingernail. "Ashley's counting on us!" A.A. couldn't imagine missing the big party. After hearing all about it for weeks, it would be a huge letdown not to be able to see it all happen. Were there really going to be tigers leaping through flaming hoops to the tune of "Happy Birthday"?

Jeanine tugged at the kimono robe she'd been lounging in all day. "I'll be glad when all this nonsense over a birthday party is over and done with. It's all you talk about. Boring!"

A.A. sighed, staring down at the chopping board. She wanted to get the cucumber slices as even as possible, just to show her mother what a dutiful daughter she was, even though she'd never used a knife and a chopping board in her life. The only people who ever touched kitchen utensils in their apartment were the maids, and Jeanine thought cooking was heating an aromatherapy neck-massage pad in the microwave.

Her mother was in a bad mood about parties today because the one she'd been to last night in a warehouse-turned-Moroccan casbah went all wrong: Another former supermodel, Jeanine's archrival, had turned up and hogged the paparazzi, showing off her new lips, cheeks, and extensions.

Jeanine couldn't stand it and came home early. That meant she was up and about all day, rather than lying in bed recovering. If she hadn't been up when Nancy Khan arrived at noon, A.A. could have come up with a quick lie to cover Lili's butt—maybe that she and Ned had gone for a jog in the park, and that they'd call as soon as they got back. Although Lili's mother might not have believed her, given that it was pouring rain outside. Oops!

"Anyway, I know why you really want to go to this party," Jeanine said, inching off her fluffy mules and stretching out on the sofa. "It's all about a boy, isn't it?"

"What boy?" A.A. was startled. Who was her mother talking about?

"That so-called boyfriend of yours." Jeanine snapped her fingers. "What's his name again?"

"Hunter." A.A. sighed; for a second she thought Jeanine might have been talking about Tri. And Tri was definitely not A.A.'s boyfriend. Never had been, never would be. No way. However often he called her—and he'd called her a lot this weekend, probably to apologize for his incredible rudeness, not that she'd answered or returned any of his calls—Tri was *persona non grata* as far as A.A. was concerned.

"I don't know if I like you dating boys so young," Jeanine complained. A.A. rolled her eyes and hoped her mother didn't see. She knew what was going on—every so often Jeanine had a fit of conscience and decided she had to be a Good Mom.

This meant pretending to lay down a new set of rules, like telling A.A. she should pick her school uniform up off the floor and not wait for the maid to do it, insisting that Ned eat green vegetables at least once a week, and giving them both long lectures on Studying Hard and Not Getting Too Serious Too Young.

Sometimes, when she got really carried away, Jeanine would announce she was going to buy a minivan so they could take family trips to the Grand Canyon or farmers' markets in Oregon. Ned and A.A. would have to go hide in their rooms until she came to her senses and drifted off for an Ecuadorian colonic irrigation. Usually this phase didn't last more than a day or two, so A.A. wasn't too worried this time.

"Actually, I'm probably breaking up with Hunter," she told her mother, and then almost dropped the knife with surprise. Where had that come from? She wasn't lying to Jeanine. But it wasn't as though she was thinking about breaking up with Hunter, or planning anything.

The words had just popped out of her mouth, and as soon as she said them, A.A. knew they were true. She liked

Hunter, but she didn't like him *that* way. A wave of relief crashed through her—she had to break up with him, sooner rather than later. It wasn't fair to him to pretend she liked him more than she did. And A.A. didn't mind going to Ashley's party without a date. Even Ashley herself was boyfriend free.

"I'm glad to hear it," Jeanine said, tucking a leather-trimmed cushion behind her head. "You have more important things to worry about right now. I mean, more important things to do. Like a little favor for your old mother."

"What?" A.A. finished slicing the final cucumber and pushed all the slices off the chopping board and into an oval, cream-colored Nigella Lawson bowl.

Jeanine's "little favors" often ended up being big pains in the neck. The last little favor was spending a whole weekend being a "fit model" for one of Jeanine's designer friends who was trying to break into teen fashion.

A.A. had to stand in a cold, drafty studio for two whole days, while people tried half-finished clothes on her, drew on her with chalk, and stuck her with pins. Ashley and Lili would have loved it, but A.A. was bored out of her mind.

"What is it?" asked A.A.

"I know how much you and Ned don't like to meet my, um, boyfriends. But I'd like you to make an exception this time," Jeanine said. "I really think Sven is the one. And I'd like you guys to meet him at dinner when he's in town next month. Can you help me convince Ned to meet him too?"

Oh. Was that it? Sure. A.A. could do that. Jeanine always thought the guy she was dating was "the One," which was why she'd been married so many times.

"Sure, Mom." And maybe if they met Sven, this famous film director Jeanine kept talking about, maybe she wouldn't talk anymore about having A.A. miss Ashley's big party.

Jeanine smiled. "Now, where's that yogurt? Doesn't that damn chef realize I'm getting older and more wrinkled by the second?"

19

WHAT MOTHERS DON'T KNOW AND WHAT DAUGHTERS DON'T TELL THEM

ILI HAD THOUGHT THAT SATURDAY WAS THE WORST day of her life, but that was before she got into her mother's car outside Max's house on Sunday.

"Ashley Olivia Li, I have never been more ashamed of you!" Her mother had always been great at multitasking, and today was no exception. She could drive and yell at the same time.

"I'm sorry, Mommy," Lili mumbled, picking at a muddy patch on her jeans. She couldn't wait to get out of these clothes and burn them. Her mother was making her sit on a copy of the *San Francisco Chronicle* so she didn't dirty the seats of the black hybrid SUV.

"You lied to me, you lied to your father, you lied to poor Mrs. Alioto. When she found out you were supposed to be there, she was beside herself with worry!"

Lili thought that was pretty unlikely. Jeanine had told her once that worrying caused lines, and that the only thing she ever worried about was losing her figure. But this wasn't a good time to argue the point with her mother.

"I didn't mean to upset everyone," Lili said in a small voice. "I just wanted to go camping."

"Camping!" Her mother sounded both amazed and sarcastic. "Since when have you been interested in such a thing? You don't like hiking. You don't like carrying things. You don't like being outside. You certainly don't like getting wet and dirty."

"No." Lili was forced to agree. She'd hated everything about the trip, apart from Max. Plus there was that whole debacle with the Bad News Bear.

The memory of the gloating faces of the Ugly Stepsisters, staring at her as her mother pulled away, would haunt her forever. They were so happy she was in trouble!

They were probably still giggling now about what a spoiled brat she was. And it was all their fault—if Jezebel hadn't "forgotten" to make arrangements with her parents to come and collect them, they would have been home in time. Instead they'd had to wait a whole hour and a half for Max's dad to turn up. Lili could swear that Jezebel had done it on purpose.

"And," said her mother sternly, her shiny helmet of

black hair making her look more warrior-like than ever, "I'm extremely disturbed by something that man said. That Alan Costa."

Lili searched her mind: What could Max's dad have possibly said? She'd been so busy trying to retrieve her belongings—and her dignity—from the back of his dad's Jeep, she wasn't really paying attention. The whole thing was just too embarrassing. Max had jumped out of the car to help her, but the long, pitying looks he was giving her just made everything worse.

"What?" she murmured, realizing that her mother was waiting for a reply, scrunching down in her seat for protection.

"He said that he hoped the weather this weekend wouldn't put you off going camping again with Max."

"Oh," said Lili, though it came out as more of a squeak. Nancy pulled up outside their house and beamed the remote at the heavy black gates. *Like maximum-security prison gates,* Lili thought, as the car turned into the driveway.

"So this is the reason, I presume, why you wanted to go camping. This *Max.*" Her mother made his name sound like a dirty word. "I presume he's a Gregory Hall boy."

"Not exactly," Lili murmured. "He goes to Reed Prep."

"That nuthouse that's trying to pass itself off as a prep school? How on earth did you meet him?" Nancy didn't sound impressed.

"He's in my French conversation class," Lili explained. "You know, with Madame LeBrun."

Nancy grunted. If Max had scored some points with her mother for taking pricey French lessons, she didn't show it. They pulled up outside the four-car garage, designed to resemble an old stable block. Lili didn't dare get out of the car yet; she didn't even unsnap her seat belt.

"Now listen here." Her mother turned to face Lili, her dark eyes intense. "From the way you look, it seems you've already been punished for this stupid, selfish adventure of yours. You could have drowned or frozen to death up there! Who goes camping in December?"

"It was horrible," Lili said, her voice quavering. It was true: She'd hated it up on Mount Tam. It was too foggy to see any views, too cold to enjoy being outside, and too wet to do anything but shiver. She was glad to be home, apart from being in the worst trouble of her life. She wished the bear *had* eaten her. The look on her mom's face was dire.

"But still, you have to realize that you can't always do what you want. What kind of example does that set for Josephine and Brennan?"

Lili was about to point out that her little sisters didn't care about anything except their acres of toys and their four-poster purple princess beds, but before she could open her mouth, she was struck by a horrible thought: Ashley's party!

Would her parents say she couldn't go? They knew this was the most important thing to her. It was the perfect evil punishment! Why, oh why, had Lili agreed to go on that stupid camping trip?

"So," Nancy continued, gathering up her Birkin handbag and opening the car door, "I'll have to discuss a suitable punishment with your father. At the very least, you will not be going anywhere but school and your other lessons for the next few weeks."

"But the party!" Lili couldn't help herself—the words just slipped out. She turned to her mother, who was still poised to get out of the car. "It's Ashley's birthday—her Super-Sweet Thirteen!"

Nancy sighed and shook her head.

"Really, Lili, you should have thought of that before embarking on this ridiculous escapade."

"Mom! I'll do anything—I'll stay in for the next year, really! I'll look after the twins! I'll do anything you want! But please let me go to Ashley's party."

Nancy's mouth twitched.

"Maybe," she said. "Maybe not. We'll see how this week goes. But one thing, young lady. I don't want to hear another word about this boy Max. You're far too young to be dating. You should be concentrating on your studies and not thinking about boys. You're not allowed to date until you're fifteen, just like your older sisters. Do you hear me?"

"Yes, Mom," Lili replied. Her mother had no idea that both her older sisters had been more than adept at dating behind their mother's back. Lili remembered watching the two of them duck out from the second-floor window to the roof and shimmy down the gutters. Then it was a quick jump to the bushes and the sidewalk, to freedom and the waiting arms of their boyfriends.

Lili looked outside her window to the street below. There was a way to get to Ashley's party. She just hoped the bushes wouldn't be too prickly.

20

A CUTE DATE IS THE MUST-HAVE
ACCESSORY TO ANY PARTY

EVEN THOUGH THE DAY WAS KIND OF COLD, Ashley wriggled into her cutest fall boating outfit—Tory Burch white pants, a Petit Bateau striped sweater, and powder blue hand-stitched Tod's deck shoes—and walked down to the marina. The rain had finally cleared, all the clouds blown out to sea by the stiff breeze. Ashley had no intention of taking her Sunfish out on such a windy day—the danger of damp pants, hello! But the marina had other attractions, namely the off chance she might spot the elusive Cooper again.

After inviting him to her party, she realized she didn't even know where to send an invitation. She thought she would drop one off at his yacht.

It had been only a few days since Ashley's parents had

dropped the baby bombshell, and she still needed time to recover. The good news: There was no more talk of her party being canceled or downsized. Matilda and Henry were so concerned about Ashley's emotional well-being, they'd capitulated on almost every detail of her Super-Sweet Thirteen. Thank goodness! Now that the entire seventh grade of Miss Gamble's was invited, it was more vital than ever to make the impression of the century. Make that the millennium.

The bad news was that Ashley still didn't have a boyfriend. All the other Ashleys would be turning up at the party with dates. Lauren even had a choice of two. But since the end of her nonromance with Tri Fitzpatrick, Ashley was alone. She was going to be sweet thirteen and never been kissed. It was pathetic. She had to do something about it, and soon.

The marina was jammed with bobbing yachts, each bigger and whiter than the next. Ashley padded down the narrow dock that led toward her family's berth, her eyes peeled for any sign of Cooper. And there he was, standing on the deck of his boat and shouting at her!

"Hey!" he called, and she resisted the urge to break into a run, even though this was exactly what she'd been hoping for. "Ashley, right? We're going out for a spin around Alcatraz—want to come along?"

Did she? That was a no-brainer. Not only was *Flown the Coop* one of the most impressive luxury yachts in the whole marina, it was the personal property of the best-looking boy she'd ever seen in her life. He was so stunning, she was a little worried he might be prettier than her.

The breeze was ruffling Cooper's dark mop, and she loved the way he was standing there, a coil of rope in his tanned hands, looking all sporty and capable and confident. Even better, apart from the uniformed captain of the yacht, visible on the upper deck, Cooper was alone. Ashley was sick of all those lacrosse jocks who just wanted to hang out together and talk about goals and defensive plays and attack positions. Yachting was an ideal sport, as in there was a driver—captain, pilot, whatever!—so all you had to do was enjoy the ride.

"I was hoping you'd come by," he admitted with a shy, crinkling-up-at-the-edges smile, reaching out a hand to help her on board. "I should have asked you for your number last time."

"That's okay." Ashley beamed. The yacht was amazing. Its three above-water decks were all gleaming steel and expensive dark wood, and there was a built-in U-shaped seating area in the stern of the boat, complete with what looked like a giant white-paneled coffee table, which turned out to be the cover of a Jacuzzi. If only Ashley had brought her bikini!

"How long can you stay out?" Cooper asked, giving her a tour of the below-deck galley and living room, explaining that there were four master berths with en suite bathrooms on the bottom deck, each named for a different island in the Pacific.

"A couple of hours—or however long you want," Ashley told him. She had a ton of homework to do, which she'd been ignoring all weekend, but that wasn't important. Her mother could write a note to Miss Gamble's, explaining that Ashley was going through a serious emotional trauma right now and couldn't possibly focus on her schoolwork. That was totally true, except the trauma was mainly about her NBK status rather than the future mini-Spencer imposed on her by her embarrassing parents. Priorities, priorities!

Cooper consulted with Captain Jack, who had a strong Jamaican accent and several gold teeth, and they promised to have Ashley back well before dark. Soon they were puttering out of the marina and into the dark open waters of San Francisco Bay, the city spreading around them like a vast arena audience.

Ashley always loved seeing the city from the water, though if she were with her parents right now, sailing on the *Matilda*, she'd be complaining about the cold wind and insisting on staying inside to watch *Tyra* reruns on the satellite TV.

But somehow, with Cooper, the ice-edged fall day seemed romantic rather than unseasonably cold. When he noticed her shivering, he produced a gray Hermès blanket to wrap around her shoulders and carried out a steaming mug of organic Guatemalan hot chocolate, which—he promised after Ashley explained her life-threatening allergy—came from an entirely nut-free mountainous region.

"This is such a great boat. It's a Lürssen, isn't it? They're the best," Ashley said, admiring the ship's sleek lines. She knew they were also the most expensive—her late grandfather had one.

Cooper shrugged. "It's just okay. So, how're things going with your mom?" he asked.

"Not great—she's pregnant. I'm going to have a baby brother or sister," said Ashley, taking a sip from her cup.

Cooper smiled. "That's cool."

"Really? Do you have brothers or sisters?"

"No, but I wish I did. It gets kind of lonely being an only child."

It was nice to speak so easily to a guy for a change. Unlike Tri, Cooper had plenty to say—talking about the history of the harbor and his favorite sailing destination (Cabo, just like hers!), as well as telling a not-too-gross story about the only time he'd ever been seasick, when they were sailing in Hawaii. Ashley sipped her hot chocolate and made sure the blanket didn't completely obscure her cute sailing outfit, snuggling down into the big, comfy cushions of the seating area.

"It's less than a week to my party," she told him. They were sailing past the craggy, foreboding presence of Alcatraz, and she snuggled closer to him. "I've been working so hard to make sure everything will be perfect."

She told him about all the circus plans—the decorations, the band, the costumes, the Chinese and Russian acrobats whom Mona Mazur had wrangled away from Cirque du Soleil especially for the occasion, even though it meant they had to interrupt world tours and cancel visits to children's hospitals.

"It sounds pretty amazing," Cooper told her, pushing up the sleeves of his gray sweater and slipping on a pair of Ray-Bans.

"You *can* come, right?" Ashley just wanted to make sure. "I brought you an invitation." Of course he was coming. He seemed much more into her than Tri had ever been. Maybe she wouldn't have to wait until her birthday party to get kissed.

"I . . . I don't know," said Cooper, taking the invitation and stuffing it into his pocket without looking at it. "I mean, I'd really like to, but . . ."

"But what?" The boat was rocking, and Ashley set her cup of hot chocolate down so she wouldn't spill any on her white pants.

"I'm not really a big party kind of guy." He gave her a rueful, totally adorable smile. She wanted to squeeze him the way she squeezed Princess Dahlia von Fluffsterhaus when her puppy had just chewed something and was looking especially cute.

"It's not a real big party," she said, backpedaling. "I mean, it's totally low-key and just a few friends."

Cooper grinned. "Uh-huh. After all you've told me, I'm surprised the mayor isn't coming."

"Actually, he is. He's my godfather."

"I kind of don't know if I'll fit in," he said.

"What are you talking about? You can't even think about missing it."

"We'll see," he said. Irritatingly, that was all he would say. She picked up her mug of hot chocolate again. The sun was getting low in the sky, and her perfect afternoon was almost over. Ashley had never met a guy like Cooper before.

He was so down-to-earth about owning this awesome boat, as if it didn't matter in the least, that he had to be a Greek oil heir or something. Only people who had money oozing out of their pores were that dismissive about having it. The fact that he was shy about coming to her party made him even more attractive. She couldn't wait to show him off to all her friends! Before they sailed back into the marina, Captain Jack gently maneuvering the long, elegant boat into the dock, Ashley had made up her mind: She had to make sure Cooper attended her birthday party.

If he wasn't there, then the whole party might as well be canceled.

21

LAUREN IS SO NOT
A *MADE* COACH

L AUREN WAS WORRIED. SHE REALLY DIDN'T KNOW if she could pull off the transformation of Sadie Graham from nerd to neo-Ashley. It was Monday already—and that meant the final countdown to Ashley's birthday party the following weekend had begun for real.

And just in case anyone had forgotten about the pending festivities, Ashley had hung a banner that read SIX DAYS TO THE EVENT OF THE SEASON. HAVE YOU RSVP'D? over the main doors of the Little Theater. She had let it slip that a certain smooth R & B crooner with the number one hit in the nation, "Baby, I Like Your Booty," was going to serenade her at the party. Half the girls in class were in love with him. By the time MOD announcements were over, the entire seventh grade at Miss Gamble's was in a state of near hysteria.

But Sadie was still playing it cool.

"It's just a stupid party," she told Lauren on their way out of the school gates that afternoon. They were walking to the optical shop so Sadie could get fitted for contact lenses at long last, after days of driving Lauren crazy with her indecisiveness. "I don't know why everyone thinks it's such a big deal."

"You'll enjoy it," Lauren wheedled, though she was almost at a breaking point with Sadie. She'd been spending almost all her time trying to whip Sadie into shape, but her friend was far from being grateful.

She complained that her new haircut, an asymmetrical long bob, with honey-golden streaks, made her look like an Afghan hound. She'd tried on more than fifty of Lauren's outfits and didn't like any of them, whining that they were all too revealing, too tight, too loose, too rough, too bright, too sheer, too patterned, or too old for her.

Then Sadie insisted that she couldn't walk in high heels, not even two-inch heels, and lectured Lauren about damaging one's feet and perpetuating dangerous female stereotypes.

Sadie was so obstinate: She wouldn't get her ears pierced, or even consider a push-up bra. Lauren was in despair. What Ashley always said was so true: You can lead a clotheshorse to prêt-à-porter, but you can't make her shrink. Something like that, anyway. Lauren's brain was fried.

Her plan was never going to work. She should have picked someone else to infiltrate the Ashleys with—maybe Sheridan or Melody. Sadie was way too much work.

It was just as well that the Ashleys were so caught up in their own lives that they hardly noticed Lauren spent more time with Sadie than with them. She was even beginning to miss them a little. The other day Ashley had the group over to meet the StripHall Queens and learn some hot new dance moves. Lauren had dearly wanted to go, but that was the same time as their meeting with the fashion stylist she'd hired to help Sadie transform from a "Don't" into a "Do." So instead of learning how to do a kick-turn-shake-shake-shake, she'd been stuck listening to Sadie complain that necklaces, stockings, and lace underwear made her itch, and that spaghetti straps dug into her bony shoulders.

Lauren wished she would just make up her mind. Why was it that when she was with the Ashleys, the girls she purported to hate, she had a lot of fun, and whenever she was with Sadie, it was like pulling teeth?

She followed Sadie into the eyeglass shop, just as a boy was stepping out.

"Christian!"

"Oh, hey!" Christian's face broke into a wide grin.

"I didn't know you wore glasses!" Lauren said.

"It's a big secret. I'm like Clark Kent," Christian admitted. He put his new spectacles on his nose, and Lauren thought he looked even cuter than ever. Then he chucked Lauren on the chin and gave her a quick kiss.

Lauren sighed happily, looking up at Christian. It wasn't until she felt a nudge on her elbow that she remembered she wasn't alone. "Right. Sorry. This is Sadie. Sadie, this is Christian."

"I'm confused. I thought your boyfriend's name was Alex," Sadie said, a little too innocently.

"Alex? Your boyfriend?" Christian looked from Lauren to Sadie and back to Lauren again.

Lauren didn't know what to do. She was trapped. She wished that she could melt into the sidewalk and disappear.

"No, she's confused . . . ," she began weakly.

"No, it's all right," said Christian quickly. "The guy who was at your house the other day, right? Alex is cool. He's a good guy. I didn't know you guys were dating, but that's okay."

Lauren felt like her tongue was stuck in her throat. Christian was being way too nice about this.

"Um, I better go. Nice meeting you, Sadie." Christian hurried away so quickly he was across the street before Lauren could speak.

"Why did you say that about Alex?" Lauren demanded. "It's not true."

It was only partially true. Alex was her boyfriend. But then so was Christian. She wondered what Christian was thinking. She felt awful that he had to find out this way. She didn't even get a chance to explain anything.

"What's the deal, then? Are you with Christian or Alex, or what?" Sadie demanded.

"Why are you being so judgmental?" Lauren huffed. None of the Ashleys ever spoke to her this way. They knew she was having a hard time of it and didn't press her or make her feel like a heel the way Sadie was doing right now.

Sadie shrugged and went to get fitted for her new contacts. "I think Alex is cuter, by the way." But Lauren wasn't listening. She decided she had to text Christian so they could really talk. But when she pulled out her phone, there was already a text from him.

L, I LIKE YOU, BUT THIS IS TOO WEIRD, he wrote. I CAN'T DEAL.

Lauren swallowed hard. She couldn't let herself cry in front of Sadie.

"What do you think of these? They're colored lenses," asked Sadie impatiently, blinking her eyes rapidly. She didn't approve of text messaging, Lauren knew. She'd told Lauren it would lead to arthritis of the thumbs. Another text message popped up.

I KNOW I NEVER ASKED U TO GO STEADY. BUT I THOUGHT I DIDN'T HAVE TO. I'M OUT. OK?

Lauren wasn't sure what Christian meant, though she had an idea. A very bleak, gray, bad idea. Like he was out of the relationship game. Like he was out of her life.

WHAT? she texted back, just to make sure, even though she didn't want to know.

SORRY. STAY FRENZ?

BFF, Lauren replied, but her hands were shaking. Now she wouldn't have to decide between Christian and Alex, because Christian had decided for her.

22

LILI IS PUT UNDER
MOUSE ARREST

ILI REALLY WANTED TO MEET THE ASHLEYS FOR their usual preparty powwow. But of course, she wasn't allowed to go anywhere. Not even to Starbucks before school! The others were sympathetic, but she could tell that Ashley was annoyed with her. Lili's decision to go camping with Max had jeopardized Ashley's happiness, because it meant all the Ashleys might not be present, lording it over the rest of the seventh grade, at her birthday party extravaganza. Luckily, Ashley was too busy obsessing over some mystery guy to be really mad with Lili.

Nancy had picked her up, as usual, and brought her home to the big mock-Tudor mansion in Presidio Heights. Lili's usual Tuesday after-class, helping a genetic researcher at Stanford in his lab, had been canceled because he had to fly to Sweden for dinner with the Nobel selection committee. So Lili had some unscheduled free time. Perfect for figuring out which outfits would be worn in what order at the party.

Instead she finished up her homework, flipped through her deck of flash cards for the ISEE's (prep-school entrance exams), and spun a few times on her Aeron office chair, wondering how she should reorganize her bedroom. It was a big room, with a huge, carved, dark-wood Chinese bed in the center, the bed piled high with red embroidered cushions. Whenever Lili was bored, she rearranged these cushions by shade and shape, and sometimes by the pattern of their embroidery. But she didn't have much enthusiasm for that today.

Her phone rang, and she snatched it up.

"Hey, Lili." It was Max. Yay! She might not be able to see him, but at least they could still talk on the phone.

"I'm so glad you called," she told him, spinning with glee in her chair. Luckily, she was safely out of the car and shut in her room. Lili didn't want her mother to find out that she and Max were still an item. No boyfriend until she was fifteen? As if! That was *years* away. That was almost college!

"I'm really sorry about this weekend," he said. She liked the way his voice sounded—sort of husky and slow. "Those doofus girls were supposed to sort out the ride home, but I should have known they'd mess up. They're both kind of flaky—not like you."

Lili smiled at the compliment. She was anything *but* flaky.

"You looked like you were in big trouble," said Max. "Sorry you got busted."

"That's okay," said Lili, trying to sound breezy. She didn't want Max to know she was virtually a prisoner in her own house.

"And we're still on for the party on Saturday, right? The guys are really looking forward to it. The Ashleys are pretty famous at our school, you know."

"Of course we're on for the party!" Lili promised. No way was she telling him her parents were still undecided about letting her go. Her father had said that if it were up to him, she'd be sent to Taiwan for the rest of the school year, to live in a boarding school run by Buddhist nuns, where girls weren't allowed any material possessions except for a gray tunic and a tin food bowl. Eeeeuch!

"LILI!" Yikes—it was her mother, calling her at top volume.

"Better go," she told Max. "Speak to you later, okay?"

"But . . . there was something I—"

"What?" Lili was curious, but her mother was roaring for her again. Not a good sign. She'd better hurry up.

"Nothing," said Max. "I mean, you'll see. Bye!"

She slipped her phone into the top drawer of her antique writing desk and rushed out to see what her mother wanted.

"You'd better get downstairs right away, Miss Lili," said one of the maids, padding along the Turkish carpet of the hallway, her arms stacked with fluffy yellow towels. "Your mother is going crazy down there."

Lili pelted down the broad staircase, past the stained-glass window on the landing, almost tripping on one of the brass carpet rods. Her mother was standing by the front door, dressed in her usual daytime-casual look of Chanel pencil skirt, TSE cashmere sweater, black pearls, and black-and-cream Chanel slingbacks.

Next to her, on the carved Korean hope chest, was a small but exquisite display of flowers. No wonder her mother was mad. Not only was the display really small—much too small for their grand dining table—but some of the flowers were white, which her mother hated. She said white flowers were for funerals. Personally, Lili thought the white snowdrops were pretty, but she knew her mother had a strict design aesthetic. Maybe she was using a new florist who didn't know her tastes?

"I thought this was the dining-room centerpiece," her mother said, looking angrily at Lili.

Whoa! It wasn't as though Lili had made it from stuff she found in the garden. Why was her mother so annoyed with *her*? "But instead I discover that these flowers are for you."

"For me?" Lili exclaimed. How cool! She'd never

received flowers before. Her mother looked less than delighted. She held up a small white envelope.

"And do you know what the card says?" Nancy's voice was icy cold. "I'll read it to you, shall I? 'To Lili—Sorry you got busted. See you Saturday—Max.'"

Uh-oh. Lili wasn't sure where to look. Part of her wanted to smile: Max had sent her flowers! Her boyfriend had sent her flowers! She couldn't wait to tell the other Ashleys!

But the rest of her knew better than to smile. After the big no-boyfriends speech on Sunday, her parents were not going to take kindly to a boy sending her flowers and talking about getting together that weekend. If she'd been in big trouble before, she was in a gigantic vat of crap now.

"It appears that even though I expressly told you not to have any contact with this boy, you defied me. We clearly can't trust you. Where is your phone?"

"In my desk drawer," Lili mumbled, shifting from one foot to the other and feeling unjustly punished. Max sent the flowers—she had nothing to do with it!

"Quintilla!" Nancy called to a young uniformed maid, who was trying to scuttle by unnoticed. "Please go up to Miss Lili's room and bring me her phone, her BlackBerry, and her laptop. You are forbidden to call or contact this boy in any way. I'm taking your phone and asking all the staff to make sure you don't use any of the house phones or computers. Until you earn our trust again, you're cut off."

E-grounded! This was the worst thing imaginable. It couldn't possibly get worse. Could it?

"And don't even think about going to school tomorrow to use your friends' phones to send messages. I'm taking you out of school for the rest of the week. I'll ask the principal to send work home for you. You are not leaving this house until we say so, understand?" Her mother had never looked so ferocious. Her Genghis side was totally showing.

Lili nodded mutely, trying to control her quivering lower lip. This was it. She had no way of getting in touch with Max. And she almost certainly wasn't going to be allowed to attend Ashley's Super-Sweet Thirteen.

There was absolutely nothing to live for. She might as well be stuck in Siberia.

23

THERE ARE SOME THINGS EVEN MONEY CAN'T BUY

ASHLEY DIDN'T FEEL LIKE GOING STRAIGHT home after school on Wednesday, and when Ashley didn't want to do something, she *wasn't* doing it. She called her mother and told her not to bother coming to Miss Gamble's at three: the Ashleys were having an after-school summit at Mel's Diner, the 1950s-style soda fountain just down the street from school.

The big house overlooking the bay was too crazy at the moment. This afternoon, the first of Mona Mazur's trucks was scheduled to pull in, so Mona could begin her total transformation of the mansion's ground floor into a circus big top.

Normally, this was the kind of thing Ashley would want to oversee and control in some way, but she had complete faith in Mona. She also didn't want to be around in case her mother, who was still suffering from morning sickness pretty much all day long, suddenly changed her mind and decided to cancel everything.

Matilda would only pull a stunt like that if Ashley were around, because she was a little afraid of Mona Mazur. So was Ashley, for that matter. So Ashley would rather steer clear until Mona had supervised the raising of the tent roof and the installation of the trapeze, by which time it would all be too complicated and too expensive to rip out.

The other reason Ashley wanted some quality time away from Chez Spencer was to discuss the Cooper situation with the other Ashleys. There were not enough hours in the day at school right now, especially with the stupid mock prep-school exams everyone was forced to study for this week. As if Ashley needed to ace a test to get into the best prep schools in the country, when one call from her dad would get the job done more efficiently.

Everyone's personal dramas were so inconvenient. Why was it all the Ashleys were moaning about boys instead of doing what they did best—helping Ashley get her way? A.A. was awash with guilt over how Hunter took their breakup, Lili'd been snatched out of school because of that stupid camping adventure, and Lauren was moping because one of her two boyfriends had dropped her. As if she didn't have another!

And if Lauren thought Ashley hadn't noticed she was secretly hanging out with Sadie Graham, Lauren had seriously underestimated the gossip grapevine. Not that Ashley was going to bring any of that up; she'd decided to keep it to herself for now and act on the information later, if needed. In the meantime, Lauren was still in the Ashleys. But Ashley relished knowing that that could change on her whim at any moment.

At Mel's Diner, her friends—minus Lili, because even a soy mocha milkshake with her gal pals was strictly verboten this week—took over the corner booth, squeezing along its red-glitter vinyl seats and drumming their French-polished nails on the silver-swirled Formica tabletop.

"This is such a cute place," said Lauren, gazing around at the individual jukeboxes on each table and the central lighting fixture, a dangling mobile made from old vinyl records. "Alex is meeting us here. He said he might bring Tri along, since they'll both be coming back from some boys' Academic Decathlon together. Is that okay?"

"Sure." Ashley shrugged, scanning her menu for nut-free organic options. Normally she would be outraged if an Ashleys summit was infiltrated, but today she thought a little male advice might come in handy. Maybe Alex and Tri knew Cooper.

"Don't the guys have some crew meet later?" A.A.

scowled. She viciously twisted one of her pigtails and stuck the end in her mouth.

"Senior team only," said Lauren, who was the expert, apparently.

"Shame," mumbled A.A. through a mouthful of hair.

Ashley stared down at her laminated menu with its polka-dot ribbon trim, making sure she didn't catch A.A.'s eye. She still felt a twinge of guilt whenever A.A. mentioned Tri.

By the time Ashley and Lauren had ordered their soy milkshakes, and A.A.—who never cared about calories—had decided on a double-chocolate malt, the boys were slouching in, both in their uniforms—shirts hanging out, ties loosened, and shoes scuffed.

Ugh! Why were boys so lazy? Before the guys arrived, the Ashleys had been checking themselves out in compact mirrors, making sure their lip gloss was fresh and their teeth were stain and food free.

Tri and Alex both ordered towering ice-cream sundaes, which was just as well—eating gave the boys something to do. Neither Lauren nor A.A. were acting very friendly toward them. A.A. was sucking down her malt and glaring at Tri, as though she was offended by his presence.

Lauren, who was supposed to be going out with Alex, seemed uncomfortable around him, as though she wished he wasn't there, though she was, at least, asking him a few bored questions about what had happened at school that day. Ashley decided to get the conversation back on track. She kicked Tri under the table, which made him spit out a chunk of banana.

"I have something to ask you," she told him, ignoring the fact that he was picking the soggy banana slice off the table and putting it back in his mouth. Ew. How could she ever have liked him? "Do you know a guy at Gregory Hall named Cooper?"

Tri thought for a moment and then shook his head.

"Nope," he said. "What grade is he in?"

"Eighth, maybe?"

"Nope. There's no one named Cooper in seventh or eighth grade. Maybe he goes to Saint A's?"

Ashley didn't think Cooper was a Saint Aloysius boy—everyone there had to keep their hair short, above their collars, and Cooper's dark hair was longish and curled beneath his ears. "Alex, do you know anyone named Cooper at Saint A's?"

Alex, his mouth full of ice cream, screwed up his face and rolled out his white-streaked bottom lip.

"I think that means no." Lauren sighed, tapping her cheek with a long spoon.

This was weird. Why wouldn't they know him? Ashley described what he looked like in detail—maybe too much detail—and both Tri and Alex smirked. They couldn't think of anyone at all who looked like that and was known as Cooper.

"Maybe he goes to Reed?" A.A. asked. She pulled out her voluminous handbag and shook some quarters onto the table for the jukebox.

Ashley shook her head. There was no way her perfect guy went to that stupid Arthur Reed Prep School for the Arts, like Lili's banned boyfriend, Max. He wasn't goth or alterno enough for that place!

"What else did he tell you?" asked Lauren, sliding some quarters across the table to A.A., who was flicking through the jukebox selections. Ashley wished everyone would focus on *her* problems for a change.

"Nothing, really." And he really hadn't. They'd talked a lot, but not about stuff like specific schools or specific addresses. Or even last names. "But he has my number—I made sure I gave it to him before I left the marina."

"Then it's just a waiting game." Alex gobbled down the last of his sundae. Tri had already finished his. Why did guys always eat as though someone was timing them? "When he gets in touch, you can ask him where he goes to school."

"Unless he doesn't call you," said A.A., shooting an evil look at Tri. "Guys do that. They're all over you one minute, and the next they've mysteriously forgotten your number."

"He'd better not forget mine," muttered Ashley, just as

the jukebox started playing "It's My Party and I'll Cry If I Want To."

A.A. wriggled out of the booth, saying something about going to the bathroom, but Ashley was too distracted to do the usual girl thing, which was to go to the bathroom en masse.

Was Cooper going to show on Saturday? Or was A.A. right? If he didn't RSVP, chances were slim. If he didn't show up, her birthday was totally going to suck, no matter how many fire-eaters they hired to line the entrance. And for once in her life, Ashley Spencer was powerless to do anything about it.

24

BYE BYE HAPPINESS,
HELLO LONELINESS

.A. SPENT WAY TOO LONG IN THE BATH-
room, retying her pigtails, curling her eye-
lashes, staring at the giant framed poster
for *Rebel Without a Cause*, and hoping that Tri would be gone
by the time she returned to the booth.

But no, she was all out of luck, as usual. Back at the table,
a new song was playing—another of her selections, Justin
Timberlake's "What Goes Around Comes Around," chosen
especially for Tri, so he'd get the message about what a lowlife
he really was—and the only person who had left was Ashley.

"She's catching a taxi home," Lauren told her. "Via the
marina to look for Cooper."

Lauren resumed her conversation with Alex, which
seemed to be some tense and serious discussion; A.A. could

catch only a little of their mumblings over the blaring music, but Alex seemed to be accusing Lauren of still being into Christian. She couldn't believe that Tri was just sitting there like a bag of flour. Couldn't he tell that Lauren and Alex wanted to be alone?

"I guess I'll be going too," she said, pulling her handbag onto the table, though nobody seemed to hear. Nobody apart from Tri, that was.

"Don't go yet," he said quickly. He fidgeted with his tie. "Could we . . . do you want to go sit at the counter for a minute? I've got something I wanted to tell you."

"Whatever." A.A. heaved a deep sigh. Just what she needed—more nastiness from Tri. It was bad enough that he hung around in her living room being a pill—his family owned the hotel where she lived, so there wasn't much A.A. could do about that.

But now he was making a nuisance of himself in a public place. She hauled herself up, dragging her bag off the table, and loped to the counter. She really didn't want to hear anything Tri had to say.

Tri asked her if she wanted another milkshake, and A.A. shook her head. He didn't have his usual scowl today, so maybe he was going to apologize for all his outrageous behavior.

"I heard that you broke up with Hunter," he told her, swinging his stool back and forth. A.A. rolled her eyes. So that was it! He wanted to gloat, or maybe lecture her about relationships. When was he going to realize that they weren't friends anymore? They were nothing to each other. Seven minutes in a closet with her didn't mean anything to him, and it certainly didn't mean he had some hold over her. Jerk!

"I'm glad you all have nothing better to do at Gregory Hall than spread gossip." A.A. clutched her bag for moral support. She'd give Tri another thirty seconds, and then she was signing out.

"What I'm trying to say is . . ." Tri looked down at the counter, clutching its rim with his long-fingered, golden-brown hands. "I wanted to tell you that I've broken up with Cecily."

"Really?" A.A. spun to face him, shocked. "But why? Cecily's great."

"You like her?" Tri seemed confused.

"Yeah! I mean, I only met her a couple of times, but she seemed nice and all. Too nice for you, anyway."

"She *is* really great," Tri agreed. "But I thought . . . I thought you'd be pleased. I kind of hoped, anyway. You know, to hear that . . ."

He trailed off, staring at the counter again, gripping it so tightly that his knuckles were turning white. A.A. didn't know where to look either. Or what to think. She'd broken up with Hunter, and now Tri had broken up with Cecily.

Both of them were free agents. They could date anyone they wanted. They could even—you know, in theory—date each other. Couldn't they? Was this why Tri had been calling her all week? Was this what he was attempting to say now? A.A. felt her cheeks grow hot. She couldn't trust herself to speak, let alone look at Tri.

"So that's it?" Someone was speaking in a really loud voice, and it took a second for A.A. to register that it was Alex. She looked back over her shoulder and saw Alex standing next to the corner booth, running a hand through his wild dark hair.

Lauren looked completely miserable. She was still sitting in the booth, hunched over the table, her head in her hands.

"I'm so sorry," she was saying over and over, but Alex wasn't calming down.

"Yeah, you should be," he announced, grabbing his backpack from the floor where he'd dumped it earlier. "See you around, Lauren. Have a nice life."

Alex marched out of Mel's Diner, clanging the door shut behind him. Lauren was still huddled in the booth. She was probably mortified, A.A. thought, because everyone else in the place was staring at her.

Without hesitation, forgetting all about Tri and his revelation, A.A. slid down from her counter stool and walked toward the booth, wishing that the jukebox wasn't playing the Everly Brothers singing "Bye Bye Love" at this very moment. It was only when she sat down on the red vinyl seat and curled a supportive arm around her friend's back that A.A. realized Lauren was crying.

25

JEANINE HAS COSMO WISDOM TO GO WITH THAT COSMO COVER SMILE

So THIS WAS HER PUNISHMENT, LAUREN realized. After flying too close to the sun, she'd got totally burned. All that double-dealing had bit her in the butt. Christian had bailed on her, and now she'd broken Alex's heart as well. She had to—it was the only fair thing to do, given the fact that all she could think about was Christian.

But it didn't make her feel any better.

"My mother might be home," A.A. warned her. They were in the private wood-paneled elevator of the Fairmont, zooming up to A.A.'s penthouse suite.

After Alex walked out on them in Mel's Diner, too annoyed to stick around any longer, and Tri had discreetly melted away, A.A. insisted that Lauren come home with her.

The diner wasn't far from the Fairmont, and A.A. said that Lauren could wait for Dex to pick her up there. Lauren felt incredibly grateful. She didn't want to sit there in the diner listening to sad old songs while all the other customers whispered about her. A.A. really *was* the nicest of the Ashleys.

The door dinged open, and Lauren was overwhelmed by the vast white apartment that opened up in front of her. Everything she could see, from the stone fireplace to the heavy silk drapes to every single piece of furniture, was a stark, snowy white. Even the beautiful woman lying flat on a chaise and reading a magazine, her dark hair cascading to the floor, was dressed completely in white—white jeans, white angora sweater, white velvet headband.

"Mom!" shrieked A.A., bounding toward the chaise and hurling her bag onto a white hide-covered stool. "What have you done?"

Jeanine Alioto dropped her magazine and stared over at Lauren, who was still lingering by the closed elevator doors.

"Who's there?"

"It's Lauren," A.A. told her, her voice impatient. "I can't believe you've redecorated *again*. We only got that raspberry sofa a couple of weeks ago!"

"I decided I'm allergic to berries." Janine craned her head, scrutinizing Lauren from head to toe. "I thought they all had to be called Ashley. Why is she hiding over there?"

"Sorry," said Lauren, inching forward. A.A.'s mother might be glamorous, but she was also kind of scary.

"Step away from the doors," Jeanine said in an imitation-robot voice. She sat up, swinging her long legs to the ground. "Hey, Lauren, do you mind if I call you something else? Your name reminds me of a certain designer who fired me from his campaign. Can you believe he thought I was too old? I'll call you Lola instead. Much better."

"Mom!" A.A. put her hands on her hips. "Don't tease her. She's had a traumatic afternoon. She had to break up with a boy and he got all mad and stormed off."

"Now that's more like it!" Jeanine flashed a brilliant smile at Lauren and patted the seat next to her. "Come sit down, Lola. This is my kind of school report. Tell me everything."

Lauren sat on the edge of the chaise, fumbling for a tissue in her pocket. All she could think of was Alex's flushed face, and the way his dark eyes flashed with anger. He thought she'd chosen him over Christian—and now he really didn't understand why she was dumping him. Everything Lauren did was just wrong. How did she get into such a muddle?

A.A. pushed her bag off the low stool and plopped down, kicking off her Louboutin Mary Janes.

"Mind the new rug!" Jeanine gave a breezy wave of her fingers. "It came all the way from Zimbabwe."

"Did it now?" A.A. asked sarcastically. "Lauren, all this looked completely different this morning when I went to school. It looked fine, perfectly fine."

"A.A., you're such a traditionalist!" Jeanine complained, rolling her eyes at Lauren. She was even taller than A.A., as long and thin as an icicle, with the same well-developed chest. "How did I end up with such boring, normal kids? It must be your father's genes."

"I'm not anything like Dad," A.A. retorted. "Did you even think about Ned eating pizza in front of the TV every night? He's going to flip when he sees this. *You're* going to spaz the first time he drops a slice of pepperoni."

"No more pizza in this place," Jeanine sniffed. "You all have to eat white food from now on. Like white asparagus . . ."

"Yuck!"

"And white truffles . . ."

"You've got to be kidding!"

". . . and white chocolate and meringues. And maybe mozzarella. Anyway, Lola, don't you think it looks seasonal? I was going for Winter Wonderland. I'm the Snow Queen. And I can tell you, it took many teams of elves working all day to get it looking like this. Something my ungrateful daughter fails to appreciate."

"It does look really nice," Lauren told Jeanine, even though her eyes couldn't focus exactly—the room was blinding white, and she was still obsessing over what had happened in the diner. Just a few weeks ago she had two boyfriends. Now she had none.

"So, Lola, tell me what went down." Jeanine crossed her endless legs, pulled her fluffy sweater over her knees.

"Maybe she doesn't feel like talking," said A.A., tugging loose her pigtails.

"It's okay," Lauren said weakly, though she didn't really know what to tell Jeanine. The whole thing sounded like one big soap opera. "I was going out with these two boys, Alex and Christian, and I couldn't decide between them."

"*Yeah*, baby!" cried Jeanine, her brilliant blue eyes sparkling. "*Now* I get why you're an Ashley! It's not enough to look cute, right? You have to want total world domination."

"Mom," hissed A.A., and Jeanine clapped a hand over her mouth, pretending to be sorry, even though her mischievous eyes told a different story. Lauren shifted uncomfortably. Maybe Jeanine could see into her soul and knew about her secret plan to topple the Ashleys. Although A.A. was being so nice right now, Lauren couldn't remember why it was she wanted to break them in the first place.

"So anyway—they found out," she continued. She couldn't believe she was telling a total stranger all about her sad love life. "They go to different schools, but it's a small town."

"Tiny," agreed Jeanine, forgetting her mock vow of silence.

"And they said I had to choose."

"Cry me a river, baby," lamented Jeanine. "Why do the dudes think it's all right for them to two-time, but the second we have more than one guy on the go, they get all clingy and exclusive? I say, dump them both."

"Well, you see," Lauren stumbled on, "then Christian, he told me he couldn't deal with it. He said we could be friends, and just to go out with Alex. So I did."

"So what's the problem?"

"The problem is, she really prefers Christian," A.A. told her mother. "That's right—isn't it, Lola? I mean, Lauren."

"I didn't realize it until Christian and I broke up." Lauren nodded. "I just couldn't stop thinking about him. I guess deep down I always liked him more."

"Usually I don't do *deep down*, sweetie, but I think I follow," sympathized Jeanine. "So tell me—if you liked this Christian so much, why did you let him go?"

Lauren shrugged.

"Maybe . . . maybe I just couldn't admit it," she confessed. "It was so much fun dating Alex as well. It was nice getting so much . . . attention. But now that it's just me and him, it's not so much fun. I wish I'd dumped Alex right away rather than wait so long. Because now Christian is probably over me, and Alex is all mad at me for leading him on."

"Love is a battlefield," Jeanine groaned.

"Mom, would you stop making lame eighties references? This is serious." A.A. squeezed onto the chaise between Jeanine and Lauren, flexing her long, narrow feet and frowning. "Guys suck. You can't trust them."

"Don't listen to her." Jeanine craned her neck to look at Lauren. "All she knows about keeping a man she learned from me, and that's not saying much. What you have to do, doll-face, is bite the bullet."

"What do you mean?" Lauren asked, dabbing at her still-damp nose with a crumpled tissue. She had to pull herself together before Dex got her and started asking pointed questions.

"You know, bite the bullet. Seize the day. Grab the moment. Round up the wagons and start shooting back at the Indians."

"Start shooting back at the *Native Americans*," A.A. corrected her.

"Whatever! Listen, do you want this guy Christian back or not?"

Lauren nodded. Of course she did. Christian made her feel so happy whenever they were together. His kisses were soft, and so was his adorable face. Even if they were just hanging out and watching a movie, it was fun. But after she'd lied to him and then kept him dangling, would he take her back? More importantly, would he take her back in time for Ashley's party?

He'd been invited, of course. Ashley had issued invitations to all the cutest guys from Gregory Hall and Saint Aloysius.

"Then," said Jeanine, examining her pearly nails as though they were a crystal ball, "you have to do the following. Listen very carefully, and promise me you'll do exactly what I say."

Lauren nodded again. She would do whatever it took. Even listen to A.A.'s mother.

26

PARTY OF ONE

FINALLY. FINALLY! IT WAS SATURDAY NIGHT, the night Ashley had been waiting for all her life—the night of her Super-Sweet Thirteen birthday party. Her real birthday was tomorrow, but it fell on a Sunday and Saturday night was so much better.

Ashley stood in her bedroom, perched on a low stool, getting sewn into the first of this evening's outfits. Maria, one of the maids, crouched at her feet, carefully stitching the hems of Ashley's sparkling jersey Wolford leggings to the ribbon trim of her ballet slippers. So there was no way she could risk something distracting and potentially humiliating, like a shoe dropping off!

Originally she'd planned to make her grand entrance on a Vespa, but Mona had persuaded her that zooming in on a trapeze would be more dramatic.

Over the leggings she was wearing a Gucci Grecian-style

tunic, made from layers of delicate chiffon, each a slightly different shade of purple. Her hair was slicked back into an elaborate chignon, interlaced with iridescent ribbon and swansdown, courtesy of the San Francisco Ballet hairstylist who'd skipped the ballet's matinee so she could spend all afternoon at the Spencers'.

The whole look was supposed to say "shimmering otherworldly goddess," flying in from another world and dropping—via a glittering silver trapeze—into the hub of the party.

Maria rocked back on her heels, prodding at Ashley's ankles with a rough fingertip.

"All finished, Miss Ashley." She sighed. "I'll be waiting here, so when you're ready to change, I can undo all the stitches."

Uh-huh. Ashley had no intention of standing around wasting valuable party time getting unstitched. Maria could just cut her out of this ensemble. What was she going to do with it afterward, anyway—donate it to an acrobat charity shop?

No, there wasn't that kind of time to waste. She had another four outfits—three gorgeous dresses and a sleek, skintight Pucci jumpsuit for her grand exit on the Vespa—hanging on closet doors, waiting to make their downstairs debut. There were only so many hours in the evening, unfortunately.

Ashley stepped off the stool, flexing one foot and then the next to make sure her legging-shoe combo was gravity-proof. A glance at the LED digital display on her Bose bedside stereo system told her it was just after seven. Guests were beginning to arrive. The sounds of excited chatter floated up from the gated front yard. She hurried over to the window and kneeled on the window seat, peering down at the arrivals through her slatted bamboo blinds. It all looked so amazing!

A dozen muscular guys, all painted surreal shades of gold and purple, stalked the yard on towering stilts, puffing billowing clouds of flame over the heads of arriving guests. Two performing monkeys darted up and down the sawdust-strewn path, weaving through the legs of incoming visitors, tumbling and springing like the cutest miniature acrobats.

Two photographers, one still and one HD video, wound through the crowd, capturing everyone's amazed reactions for posterity. Ashley had wanted an elephant to be performing tricks out there as well, but the permit got held up at city hall. Typical! She tried to talk her father into flying in an elephant from the San Diego Zoo—she was sure they had a few extra they wouldn't miss for a night—but he was too busy cooing at her mother's belly and meeting with the Hopi Indian craftsman who was hand-carving the new baby's crib out of bleached whalebone and willow sticks to lift a finger about Ashley's eleventh-hour wildlife crisis. Double typical!

At the gated entrance, William, the dignified, silver-haired family butler, dressed in a lion suit, held a walkie-talkie behind his back and stood next to Silvana, the prettiest of the Spencers' maids. These two family retainers had extremely important jobs tonight. Silvana, dressed (semi against her will, though she should have been grateful) in a tight-fitting assistant ringmasteress costume, complete with fishnet tights, a red jacket, and a jaunty black silk top hat, was holding a Palm Pilot, its screen revealing a miniature master copy of the guest list. She checked off names as guests arrived, announcing each person to William.

His job was simple. As soon as Cooper arrived, the butler was to call Ashley on his cell phone. Then, and only then, would she prepare to make her grand entrance. She wished she knew Cooper's last name. All she'd been able to tell Silvana was that Cooper was around fourteen, super hot, and possibly a Greek oil tycoon's heir.

Silvana had rolled her eyes at Maria—Ashley totally saw her!—and asked if he'd be wearing a toga. Either Silvana was incredibly ignorant or this was some kind of Honduran in-joke. Cooper better not be wearing a toga! Actually, Ashley didn't really care what he was wearing, as long as he turned up.

When she'd gone to the marina the other day to look for him, *Flown the Coop* had lived up to its name. The boat was gone. She'd stared at its empty berth for a while, then kicked a coil of rope lying on the deck in frustration. But even if he'd never even RSVP'd, he had to be there tonight. He just *had* to.

But seven turned into seven thirty, and still no Cooper. William looked up at the window a few times—or at least his giant lion's head turned in her direction—and gave a mystified shrug of his furry shoulders. The yard went from thronged with wowed guests to almost empty, as everyone moved inside to be wowed all over again by the big-top interior and the acrobats zinging about overhead. Soon it was seven forty-five, and the fire-eaters were climbing off their stilts and lolling about on the lawn, drinking cans of Red Bull. Her mother was knocking at the door, saying that everyone was asking where the guest of honor was hiding.

Ashley really couldn't wait any longer. She called William, hoping that Cooper had arrived without her noticing. Maybe William had forgotten to call. Maybe Silvana had withheld vital information from him, just because she was annoyed that the top hat was flattening her bouffant hair.

"Not yet," William mumbled into the phone; it was hard to talk, Ashley supposed, when you were dressed as a lion, especially with the wind blowing your mane into your mouth. "But we'll stay here until he arrives."

"Thanks, William." Ashley sighed. At least someone was looking out for her.

"Darling!" Her mother flew into the room, a dazzling smile lighting up her beautiful face. Ashley was *so* glad she'd managed to talk Matilda out of dressing like a clown. Just because she was pregnant didn't mean she was balloon-shaped just yet. Matilda looked glam in her sexy tiger outfit, like a cuddlier version of Catwoman, her blond hair pulled back into a swinging ponytail, little tiger ears perched on her head.

"I'm ready, Mommy," Ashley said, submitting to a make-up-smudging kiss, and only half listening while her mother reminded her that the city's health and safety inspector needed to make sure she was thoroughly harnessed before permitting any acrobatic descent.

She looked down at the crowd gathered below. So many people were there—the mayor and his pretty new wife; several stars of that irritating movie about a group of campers who put on a musical; the Sugar network's cameramen, who were stationed in every corner. All the old San Francisco families were represented too. Every girl in her seventh-grade class was probably sick with envy and admiration. But no Cooper. He hadn't bothered to show up.

This was supposed to be the happiest day of her life.

But Ashley could barely even manage a smile.

27

THE ASHLEYS ARE PRETTY
IN PURPLE

A.A. HAD TO HAND IT TO ASHLEY—THIS WAS the best party ever. Not a single detail had been overlooked. From the unicycle-riding waitresses with their pink cotton-candy wigs to the master of ceremonies cracking his whip at the front door, the event was totally on-message. Even the canapés were themed. So far A.A. had scarfed down five meatballs shaped like miniature seals and two pastry-case gypsy caravans, filled with mini seafood "lions." And she was still only in the lobby.

She pushed her way through the crowd, looking for the other Ashleys. A.A. was wearing a slim column dress and sparkly sandals. After the prebirthday shopping trip, they'd declared a dress truce and agreed that they should all wear a shade of purple this evening.

This would mirror the color of Ashley's first outfit of the night and complement all the other changes she had planned. Lili had dropped the issue of the red velvet dress when Lauren pointed out she might look too much like the red velvet rope sectioning off their private dance floor. Just as well—A.A. was tired of all the arguments. This party might be amazing, but she'd be relieved when all the craziness was over.

A.A. wriggled through a gaggle of Miss Gamble's seventh graders, all talking at the top of their voices and gazing around Ashley's house as though it were the White House. They'd never been here before, of course. They probably thought she had a pink lemonade fountain—spraying out of a giant hose, held by a carved ice-cream clown—in her living room all year round.

Where was Lili? And where was Lauren? A.A. couldn't walk around being fabulous alone. Soon she was going to be sucked into some lame interview with Guinevere Parker, who was standing in one corner, dressed in a *hideous* puce taffeta prom dress from hell and round-toed flats, muttering into a handheld tape recorder.

Maybe she was writing a story about the party for the Miss Gamble's newspaper—or maybe she had nobody to talk to apart from a machine. A.A. almost took pity on her—almost—and then hurried by. One advantage of being so tall was that you could pretend you didn't notice somebody lurking a foot or two below your sight line.

A.A. had worries of her own right now, anyway. It wasn't at all certain that Lili would be here tonight. They had no idea what was going on with her—she didn't come to school and didn't answer her phone, e-mails, or IM, which meant she was probably in the worst trouble ever with Genghis Khan.

A.A. had been inside the house for twenty minutes, and there was no sign of Lili at all. The party wouldn't be as much fun without her. Ashley was going to be all preoccupied with this Cooper dude, not to mention her numerous changes of costume. Lauren was all down-at-the-mouth about losing two boyfriends in one week—not that she was anywhere in sight either. A.A. missed the good old days of the Ashleys, when they all went everywhere together. Boys ruined everything.

Speaking of boys . . . she couldn't stop thinking about Tri. A.A. hadn't seen or heard from him since the other day in the diner, when he told her he'd broken up with Cecily. What was she supposed to say? Why had he made such a big deal about telling her? It was all totally mystifying.

Maybe he had other stuff he wanted to tell her, but that wasn't possible on Wednesday: Lauren was all upset, and A.A. had felt so bad for her. Tri had backed off, saying he and A.A. could talk about stuff another time. So why the sudden silence? Was the "another time" he had in mind sometime years in the future, like when they were in high school?

"A.A.!" Someone was calling her name, and she turned around slowly, dreading what—or who—she might see. There, stranded on the far side of the ice-cream clown, surrounded by a twittering bunch of Miss Gamble's girls, was Tri.

Her heart clenched—much to her annoyance. So Tri was at the party; who cared? It was no big deal. She knew he'd be here. What she *didn't* know was that he'd look so . . . well, so hot. He was wearing a crisp white button-down shirt, a navy blazer, and pressed chinos. Were her eyes blinded by all the circus lights? Because he didn't even look at all short.

A.A. decided the best policy was to avoid him. Hot or not, Tri was trouble. She was never sure if he liked her or despised her. And if she wanted to live her life on an emotional roller coaster, she'd just spend *all* her time with the other Ashleys.

She spun on her pointed Jimmy Choo heel and tried to head toward the sunroom, where she'd heard there were dogs jumping through hoops over mounds of hot coals or something. But the crush of the crowd slowed her progress, and the next thing she knew Tri was next to her, pulling on her arm.

"Hey!" he shouted. "Over here!"

He gestured with his head to a relatively deserted corner near the giant lion's cage where the band would be playing

later on. A.A. shrugged and allowed herself to be pulled away. The dogs-jumping-over-coals could wait. Tri seemed like he was bursting with something to say, and that made her feel like *she* was jumping over coals. She wished he didn't have that power over her, the power to make her feel anxious and weird and skittish.

"I've been looking for you everywhere," Tri told her when they were both wedged against the bars of the cage. He was standing very close to her.

"Why?" A.A. asked.

He leaned close to her, his deep blue eyes fixed on her intently. A.A. couldn't move. She could barely breathe. This was it. What was Tri going to say?

28

BIG-TOP BUST-UP

".A.!" LILI WAS SO EXCITED TO SPOT HER friend in the corner, by the giant empty lion's cage. She felt as though she'd been living in a sensory deprivation tank for the last few days, denied all gossip, chitchat, and backstabbing. What kind of a life was that? Her parents might as well have sent her to the threatened Buddhist boarding school. She was bursting to talk to someone other than her pillow collection.

She pushed through the crowd, eager to reach A.A. and . . . who was that with her? Tri? Wow, he looked really cute. He didn't even look as short as he used to be.

She was so lucky that her mother had finally relented about the party—mainly thanks to a call from Ashley's mother, who said that Ashley had been crying all afternoon because Lili wasn't going to be there. At first Lili was touched. Ashley crying because she couldn't come—really?

Then she came to her senses. The last thing Ashley wanted was puffy red eyes at her party. She'd probably talked—or browbeaten—her mother into making the call. But Nancy Khan didn't know that, did she? Lili's mother had stood there in her bedroom, arms crossed, and said that Lili was allowed to go for two hours only, just as a favor to Mrs. Spencer, and that she had to remain under her father's supervision at all times. Nancy would have gone herself, except she had to chair a benefit dinner that night.

Lili agreed, of course. In theory, it was a drag having to come with her dad. In reality, it was no problem at all. He was so busy eating circus-themed canapés and discussing the value of his Google shares with Ashley's dad, he barely noticed Lili slipping away into the living room. It would have been much harder to escape Nancy's clutches!

Still, Lili had to make the best possible use of her freedom, just in case her dad remembered he was supposed to be watching her like a hawk rather than stuffing his face and socializing. And in that time she needed to (a) talk her head off with the other Ashleys, (b) show off her gorgeous outfit to all the Miss Gamble's plebes, and (c) find Max.

He was going to be here tonight, and he was probably mad as anything with her. The last conversation they'd had was right before the flowers were delivered. Since then he hadn't heard a peep from Lili. He'd probably called and sent text messages, none of which she'd been able to get or respond to. Maybe he thought Lili was dumping him—she had to find him and explain everything, ASAP.

"Hi, pretty!" A.A. greeted her with smacking air kisses, her cheeks kind of flushed. Tri nodded at her briskly, looking a little annoyed. Uh-oh! Maybe she was interrupting something?

"I haven't missed Ashley's big entrance, have I?" Lili was breathless with excitement about being back in the real world again. A gymnast in a glittery leotard pedaled by on his unicycle, swooping his tray under her nose. "She'll kill me if I missed the special moment."

"Don't worry—nothing's happened yet," A.A. told her, shouting over the noise of the crowd. "I don't know what the holdup is. But this whole place is such a . . . well, a circus! I haven't even seen Lauren yet."

Lili scanned the packed room, looking for Max. A.A. and Tri weren't talking now. They both seemed kind of uncomfortable.

"I'll see you guys later, okay?" Tri was already walking away, acting all bored with their company.

"Where's his girlfriend?" she asked A.A. as soon as Tri was out of earshot. "What was her name—Celery?"

"They broke up."

"Already?"

"You know what guys are like." A.A. shrugged. She pulled a lip gloss from her Celestina clutch and reapplied a thick, glossy coat. "One minute they're into you and the next . . ."

"Don't remind me," groaned Lili. "I'm afraid Max is already over me. I haven't been able to speak to him for days. You haven't seen him, have you?"

"Maybe he's in the sunroom? Or there's always the dining room," suggested A.A., jabbing to the nearby double doors. "You want to check it out?"

Lili nodded, grabbing A.A.'s hand, and together they sidled through the crowd toward the dining room. It felt like Ashley had invited all of the Bay Area, not just the entire seventh grade. And for every Miss Gamble's girl, there were at least two boys. Just not the boy she was looking for. . . .

A.A. walked ahead, and Lili lost her in the crowd. She was sidetracked because inside the ash-floored dining room, with its mission-style table and ornate Spanish sideboard, and the hand-smelted iron candelabra from Chile, she finally spotted someone she knew.

Not someone she liked, or someone she was particularly looking forward to seeing. It was that stupid Cassandra, wearing a black tutu over striped leggings, her red bangs gelled into a spike. And that insufferable Jezebel was there as well, in a black leotard and skinny vinyl jeans, smearing something disgusting into her mousy mop. Hello, was this *What Not to Wear*?

Bent double laughing were Max's idiot friends, Quentin and Jason, both looking like total posers in old tuxedo jackets worn over matching Che Guevara T-shirts. Lili's blood started to boil. She would never have invited them if she'd known they were going to be all "ironic" and irritating. Hadn't she suffered enough last weekend? And wait a second—what was that thick red and white stuff smeared all over Cassandra's Doc Marten boots? Could it be . . . no, it couldn't! It couldn't be—Ashley's cake?

Lili caught Quentin's eye, and he stopped laughing. In fact, he looked as guilty as hell. She was so livid she couldn't speak. She couldn't believe that they'd started eating the cake already, before Ashley had a chance to make her grand entrance, change into three more outfits, and cut the stupid thing. Even worse, were they really having some kind of childish *food fight* with it?

"Ah, we're really sorry, Lili," said Quentin, wiping his cake-smeared fingers off on his old jacket. "It was Jason's fault."

"It totally was not!" protested Jason. He choked back a laugh and looked sheepishly at Lili. "It was just an accident, okay?"

"What was an accident?" Lili asked icily, tapping one foot on the ground. "Hmmm? Cutting yourself a slice of cake before we've even had a chance to sing 'Happy Birthday' to the guest of honor? Acting like you're five years old?"

"I think what he means," smirked Cassandra, who didn't

look sorry at all, "is . . . well, you can see for yourself."

She and Jezebel stepped aside, like tattered curtains pulling away from a stage, and Lili realized what the red-crested nitwit was talking about.

Ashley's four-tier big-top cake, with its red-and-white-striped icing, gold-leaf tent ropes, flame-thrower candles, and three-inch incredibly realistic model of Ashley swinging on a trapeze—described by the birthday girl herself in glowing, obsessive detail at lunchtime on Monday—was lying upside down on the floor in a sorry, saggy heap, Princess Dahlia von Fluffsterhaus gobbling huge mouthfuls of its mashed-up edges.

"It really was an accident, and I'm . . ." Quentin was talking on and on, but all Lili could hear was the loud buzzing in her ears.

The cake was a total eyesore and beyond repair. She was furious with Max for having such annoying friends, furious with herself for inviting them, and furious with them for maliciously—she was sure—knocking the cake to the ground. But whoever's fault it was didn't matter now. Even if the cake had leaped off the table and onto the floor, one thing was certain.

Ashley was going to *freak*!

29

FALLING IN LOVE OR GETTING BURNED? IT'S ALL THE SAME THING

AUREN WAS A GIRL WITH A MISSION. SHE BARELY even registered the way the Spencer mansion was decorated with thousands of multicolored lights, like a giant version of the Rockefeller Center Christmas tree. She bolted past the stilt-wearing flame-eaters, hurdled over a forward-rolling monkey—not easy in delicate four-inch silk Blahniks—and practically knocked the whip out of the ringmaster's hands.

It wasn't because she was late—not *really* late, anyway. From all the shrieking chatter around her from overexcited party guests, she could work out that Ashley had yet to make her big entrance.

But she wasn't worried about missing Ashley's big moment. She wasn't even that worried about Ashley missing *her* big moment—i.e., the unveiling of the brand-new, made-over, Super-Sweet Sadie to her soon-to-be-brand-new friends, the Ashleys.

Sadie had sent her a text saying she would be there soon; she was just waiting for her escort to arrive. WHAT ESCORT? Lauren had asked, but there was no reply. This made her intensely nervous. She hoped Sadie wasn't going to blow it by turning up with some nerd doofus who'd presented her with a wrist corsage to match his nylon cummerbund!

She'd wanted them to arrive together, all dolled up and looking like a million dollars—which was about what it had cost to get Sadie party-ready. But Sadie had begged off, saying she would just meet her there. That was okay—Sadie could take care of herself for the moment, because Lauren had a far more important task to accomplish tonight.

She had to find Christian.

A.A.'s cool mom, Jeanine, had told her exactly what she needed to do. The first thing was to look unbelievably hot. Lauren glanced at her reflection in the enormous Louis Quinze mirror hanging in the expansive front hall—not an easy thing to do when you were getting jostled by hundreds of other partygoers, waiters on unicycles, and a performing iron man who kept lifting unsuspecting (and shrieking) guests into the air and dangling them from one of his giant fists.

She'd kept to the all-purple theme, as agreed, but she still felt confident about standing out from the crowd. Her dress was a light lavender color, with frayed hems and a daring neckline. Even Dex, who'd dropped her off, whistled when she walked out to the car, and told her that she looked like one hot tamale—though he immediately tried to make a joke of it, saying that she really looked like a very expensive grape, or possibly just a skinny eggplant.

Even that was praise, coming from sarcastic, cynical Dex. This was the person who'd told her he'd rather have his toes tattooed than go to what he called Ashley's spoiled-brat-a-thon. Not that he was invited: Ashley wasn't into older guys.

Anyway, the second piece of advice from Jeanine was: Find the object of your affections but don't acknowledge him. Parade up and down someplace where he can't avoid spotting you, but play it cool. No smiling, no chatting, no flirting, and absolutely, definitely, no begging to be taken back. This particular task was going to be harder to accomplish, Lauren knew. She was afraid that the second she saw Christian, she'd just run right up to him screaming, "I broke up with Alex! I broke up with Alex!"

And that, according to A.A.'s mother, would be a disaster. She said that guys like a challenge, and that he had to think he was winning Lauren back.

Lauren wasn't so sure about this. Christian was the one

who'd dumped *her*, after all: maybe he had no intention of ever winning Lauren back. But she couldn't obsess about this for another second; the main thing was to find him and do the parading up and down. Maybe her sheer chiffon dress and her shiny new pageboy do would win him over. He'd liked her once upon a time, right?

The living room was insane, packed with people gazing up to the mezzanine and its high-wire trapeze. Lauren squeezed her way through, standing on her tiptoes to try and spot Christian. She saw lots of boys, lots of boys who almost looked like Christian, and lots of boys who were inferior to him in pretty much every way—but unless he was one of the guys in bear masks tumbling over the coffee table, Christian himself didn't appear to be in the room.

She fought her way to the sunroom, almost scorching her Miu Miu wristlet purse on one of the rings of fire. Still no Christian! Maybe he was out in the backyard? Lauren pushed through the French doors, but all she could find were animal pens, catering vans, a fire truck, and a Red Cross station where exhausted unicyclists went to rehydrate during their mandatory breaks.

This was a disaster! If Christian wasn't here, how was she going to march in front of him looking sassy and cute and irresistible? Lauren stomped back into the sunroom, so down about the state of her love life that she stepped on one of the ruffle-collared terriers about to make a leap over a burning coal pit.

The dog yapped with irritation, and Lauren lost her balance, almost falling over. One of her heels caught in the gap between two slate tiles, and with a sickening *snap!* it sheared right off. Lauren let out an involuntary shriek and started tumbling into the fire pit. *Eek!*

The last thing she needed was coal burns on her hands and an evening spent being the most overdressed girl in purple at the ER. Luckily, someone grabbed her by the elbow and yanked her out of the danger zone—a little too vigorously, because Lauren, still wobbling on her broken heel, found herself staggering headfirst into a pillar and hitting her head with a bang. *Ouch!*

"Are you okay?" someone asked, and Lauren, woozy and disoriented, nodded. Better a concussion than burns, she guessed, tears of pain and embarrassment pricking her eyes. This whole house was a giant hazard.

"Sorry—I mean, thanks," she said, rubbing her head, not caring about messing up her perfect hairdo. She was going to have a nasty bump there in the morning.

"Maybe we should go to the kitchen and ask for a bag of frozen peas?"

"Yeah, maybe." Lauren fumbled in her bag for a tissue. She didn't want a stranger to see her crying.

"It doesn't feel too bad," the stranger reassured her, his hand gently pressing the crown of her head. "I mean, I think you'll live. You might suffer irreparable brain damage, but I think you'll be okay."

Lauren looked up, her breath catching in her throat. She would recognize that deadpan delivery anywhere. This wasn't a stranger. It was Christian!

"It's fine, really," she managed to squeak, reaching down to pull off the broken shoe. "I just feel kind of stupid."

"You sure were in a big hurry," he told her, his eyes boring into hers. Lauren's heart went *ker-plunk*. He was just goofy old Christian, in a button-down yellow shirt and rumpled khakis, his green eyes sparking, his dark blond hair smelling clean and apple-ish. But she was so happy to see him that all of Jeanine's advice went out the window.

"I was looking for you," she blurted. Then she didn't know where to look, so she reached down to tug off the other shoe. She'd have to spend the party barefoot—oh well!

"I was looking for you, too," said Christian, his face suddenly anxious. "I wanted to tell you—I don't care. I mean, I just kind of miss you . . . so I don't mind if you don't want an exclusive relationship, that's cool. . . ."

"No!" she practically yelled, and Christian looked startled. Luckily, everybody else was too preoccupied with the stupid dog tricks and a rogue piece of white-hot coal that was rolling out of its pit and scorching the sunroom floor. "I mean, I *do* want an exclusive relationship. You were right last week—this is too hard."

Christian's face fell.

"Okay," he said slowly. "Well, I hope you and Alex are, you know, happy. . . ."

"Not me and Alex!" Lauren realized that Christian was getting the wrong message. This bump on the head had turned her into a burbling fool! "I broke up with him this week. Didn't you know?"

"Nope." Christian shook his head, but he was smiling now.

"So, can we . . . ?" Lauren felt shy all of a sudden.

"You mean . . . me and you?" Christian looked all red as well.

"Yeah, if that's . . . you know, okay."

"Oh, it's okay," he agreed, and then they stood there, not sure what to do next. Lauren wished he would kiss her or something, but then she wished he wouldn't, because they were in such a public place, and she wanted the first kiss of their new relationship to be something amazing and special, without any jumping dogs, burning hoops, or dangerous fire pits anywhere in sight.

"Hey." He nudged her. "Speak of the devil, right? *He* didn't waste any time."

Lauren spun around and looked toward the living-room

entrance. Christian was right: There was Alex, looking darkly handsome. And hanging on his arm was a stunning girl whose piercing blue eyes surveyed the room with haughty displeasure.

Her golden blond hair was gathered in loose waves and rippled like sunshine over her bare shoulders, and a killer red minidress halted at midthigh, the better to show off her bronzed calves. On her feet were six-inch YSL stilettos, the kind you could only order from the flagship store in Rome.

Lauren knew this even though she couldn't see the girl's feet, just as she knew those blue eyes were the result of colored contact lenses, and just as she knew the oh-so-casual hairstyle had taken three hours to perfect.

She knew all this because the girl on Alex's arm was Sadie Graham.

30

SOME KIND OF
NOT-SO-WONDERFUL

A.A. WAS ABOUT TO JUMP OUT OF HER SKIN with nerves. What was Tri going to say to her? He'd just started to tell her whatever it was he was desperate to communicate, and then Lili arrived. Instead of hanging around until Lili rushed off a few minutes later to look for Max, Tri sulked and wandered away.

So now A.A. was in a state of total anxiety. If he wanted to ask her out, why not just do it? *JUST DO IT!* she felt like screaming. Why was it so hard for him to say?

And now A.A. was trapped in the living room, waiting for Ashley to make her extremely late grand entrance. From her vantage point by the vintage lion's cage, A.A. could see Ashley getting snapped and buckled onto the trapeze. Any second now she was going to whiz through the air, swing back and forth high above everyone's heads, and then get lowered onto a throne held in place by four contortionists using only their toes to keep the chair steady. Ashley had told them all about it; she'd been rehearsing for days.

"ASH-LEY, ASH-LEY, ASH-LEY!" everyone in the living room was chanting, even the unicycle-riding waiters. Up on the high mezzanine, Ashley sat on the trapeze, a huge smile on her face, accepting the adoration of the crowd.

"And now!" roared the ringmaster MC, cracking his whip so hard that everyone jumped. "Please welcome the guest of honor, the birthday girl herself, the most *extrrrrraaaaooordinary* young lady to grace the high wire . . . Miss Ashley Spencer!"

"Yay!" A.A. cheered as loudly as she could, clapping her hands above her head. Ashley was pretty brave, soaring through the air on what was, essentially, a swing seat. One giant *whoosh*, and there went Ashley—toes pointed, Grecian tunic flowing, swinging back and forth across the great room like a dainty fairy.

Guinevere Parker was so entranced by the sight, she dropped her tape recorder on the floor without even appearing to notice, and Cass Franklin had to pull out her portable oxygen tank to stop herself from hyperventilating.

"Pretty over-the-top, huh?" Tri reappeared, wriggling up close to her and leaning against the iron bars of the cage.

A.A. pretended to be watching Ashley getting lowered onto her foot-held purple throne, but her heart had started thudding loud and hard again.

"Literally," she said, trying to sound as breezy as possible. A.A. didn't want Tri to think she'd just been standing here waiting for him, even though that was pretty much the truth. "As in, she's over our heads."

"So, you know what I was trying to tell you earlier?" He leaned close to her, and A.A. wished—not for the first time in her life—that she wasn't wearing such high heels.

"Yeah?" she sniffed. She thought of the advice her mother had given Lauren: Play it cool, don't show them you're desperate, act like they're no big deal. Even when you feel the exact opposite. This was it: the moment of truth. Tri was going to tell her he'd liked her all along, and that he wanted her to go out with him. Yikes!

"I wanted to tell you," Tri said, lowering his voice so much she had to bend over to hear him. "I've been looking around the house, and I found the TV with the Wii attached. It's in the den. I didn't want to say anything in front of Lili in case she made a big deal about us playing a game when we should be dancing or something. But I knew you'd be into it, right?"

"Oh, sure." Now A.A. had to struggle to sound enthusiastic.

"Great!" Tri gave her a huge grin. "I can't wait to whip you at Black Dragon. I'll go get it set up. Do you want to grab some sodas? Get enough for four, because I'm going to round up some of the guys."

A.A. nodded mutely, trying to keep a false smile fixed on her face. So that was Tri's big news.

It was not: Wanna go out with me? Instead it was: Wanna play? Oh well. They were back to the way things used to be, she guessed. Not boyfriend and girlfriend. Not enemies. Just friends.

Maybe that was all they were supposed to be, and it was time A.A. accepted it.

"Excuse me!" A.A. began her slow march through the crowd, looking for the drinks table. She'd do just as Tri said—pick up a few sodas, then make her way to the den. Playing a few rounds of Black Dragon might be fun.

But somehow, she didn't feel much like *fun* anymore.

31

YOU CAN'T FIX A BROKEN
HEART. OR A BROKEN CAKE.

LILI NEEDED TO TAKE A BREAK. SHE'D SPENT THE
last ten minutes on her hands and knees, helping the
cleaning staff pick the remains of Ashley's cake
off the floor and attempt to reassemble it on the table. It
was a total lost cause, but they had to try something.

All the big-top cake resembled now was a deflated red-
and-white-striped beach ball. The feet and legs of the miniature Ashley had been chomped by Princess Dahlia von
Fluffsterhaus, so Lili perched the remaining half on the top
of the beach ball, letting the gilt ropes hang from the figure's
little arms.

She looked like Houdini trying to make an escape. Lili
sighed—what else could be done? Ashley was still going to
have an almighty nervous breakdown, but the majority of

guests wouldn't know the cake had spent way too much quality time on the floor.

All of Max's idiot friends had disappeared, and Lili
hoped they'd had the decency to leave the premises. She
hadn't even gotten the chance to ask them about Max, but
that didn't matter—she'd given up on finding Max here
tonight. He probably decided to blow the party off, and sent
his pathetic posse instead.

"Young lady, you're covered with frosting!" Her father
had finally managed to track her down. Really, he was a hopeless guard dog! She gave a quick explanation about the cake,
leaving out the part about the total guilt of Max's friends.

The name "Max" was a dirty word in the Li household
this week. "You should go get cleaned up," he told her,
pointing to the powder room off the front hall. "The dancing's starting, and we can only stay one more hour, okay?"

Lili scampered off to the powder room, eager to clean the
sticky mess off her hands. If she only had one more hour
here, she had to make the best of it. After Ashley got changed
into outfit number two, they were all supposed to meet at the
VIP Ashleys-only dance floor right in front of the cage. It
wasn't exactly a romantic evening with Max, but it was better
than nothing.

The line for the powder room stretched all the way to the
front yard, so Lili darted in the opposite direction, heading

down a narrow hallway toward the kitchen. The Spencer staff knew her and would let her into the bathroom there, especially because she'd helped them semi-fix Ashley's demolished cake. She held her disgusting hands up in the air, resisting the temptation to eat the moist cake crumbs trapped underneath her fingernails, and rounded the corner at high speed.

Oops! She almost crashed into someone sloping along, hands in pockets, not watching where he was going.

Max.

"Omigod!" she squealed, planting a sticky hand directly on his shoulder before she realized what she was doing. He stared with distaste at the red and white residue. "I've been looking for you everywhere! Do you know what your friends did? They wrecked Ashley's cake!"

"So what." He shrugged.

"So what?" Lili was incensed. Max was acting as if he was mad at her, when she had every right to be mad at him.

"I don't care about some stupid cake. And by the way, nice to see you, too." He frowned and began to walk away. She couldn't understand it. Then it dawned on her that Max thought she'd been avoiding him all week, when the exact opposite was true.

"Hey! Wait! Max—forget about the cake. I wanted to tell you I've been wanting to thank you for the flowers, but I've been grounded all week and I couldn't call you or anything," she babbled, almost in one long breath. "I missed you so much!"

"Sure," he said, and continued to walk back toward the party. "Whatever."

"Max—I'm telling you the truth!" Lili pleaded. "My mom and dad took my phone and everything—I wasn't even allowed to go to school!"

"That's not what I heard," Max said in a chilly voice, not even turning to look back at her. "I heard you thought the camping trip was the worst thing that ever happened to you in your life! Cassie and Jez said you bitched and moaned the whole time about having to sleep outdoors, and that you totally hated the whole thing."

Okay. So that was kind of true. Maybe she shouldn't have shot her mouth off at the Evanescence twins. Especially since they were using it against her. They wanted her out of the picture and were only there to sabotage Ashley's party. She wanted to strangle both of them with their own stringy hair.

"Max!" She scrambled after him, but he had already disappeared into the crowd in the lobby. The only guy she could see was her father, looking for her in the powder-room line.

"Would someone mind letting my daughter cut in, just to wash her hands?" he was asking, and Daria Hart, who was next in line, started waving and smiling at Lili. She probably thought this meant they'd be besties on Monday. As if!

Lili couldn't even manage a grateful smile. She slipped into the powder room and rinsed the congealing cake off her hands in the tiled Moroccan sink. Her hands were shaking so badly it was hard to get soap on them.

Max hated her. He never wanted to see her again.

32

ROMEO AND JULIET DON'T HAVE ANYTHING ON THESE TWO

"YES!" TRI THREW DOWN HIS CONTROL STICK in triumph and rocked back on the leather sofa. He'd beaten A.A. in Black Dragon. In fact, he'd beaten everyone—the other two Gregory Hall boys who'd managed to sneak into the den were his first opponents, because A.A. had been slow joining the secret party. She'd been dancing with the other Ashleys in their VIP area, even though it was difficult to dance to burlesque rockabilly when you were wearing a tight dress.

And though the VIP area was a cool idea, in reality it wasn't so much fun. Ashley danced facing the rest of the room, preoccupied with spotting the mysterious Cooper. Lauren was so busy fluttering little waves at Christian that she kept flubbing the choreographed steps—plus, without any shoes she looked kind of weird.

Lili had run in whispering something about "cake" and "disaster" as well as "Max," "break up," and "life over." Ashley soon left to deal with the cake crisis, Lili looked depressed and didn't want to talk, and Lauren and Christian were in their own world, so A.A. had headed straight to the den, as promised, with a stack of soda cans and a handful of red-and-white-striped straws.

She'd played a couple of rounds, and then there was a huge commotion from the party and the other guys went to check out what was happening—probably just Ashley getting her birthday gift in the front yard.

That left just two of them in the den—A.A. and Tri. She gurgled the last of her soda and told Tri she didn't feel like playing another game.

The whole evening felt really flat. She didn't even care about getting beaten by Tri—she wasn't making much effort, so it really didn't count. He seemed to sense her strange mood.

"What's up?" he asked, tapping her on the arm with his soda can.

"Nothing." She shrugged. She didn't have the energy to get up and rejoin the party. Maybe she should just call the Fairmont driver and go home. Tri sat his empty can on the coffee table and turned to face her.

"You know the other day in the diner?" he asked her, his voice quiet and serious. "I was trying to tell you something."

"About breaking up with Cecily, I know." A.A. leaned her feet against the edge of the table. These shoes were killing her.

"Yeah, but I also wanted to explain what happened with Ashley a while back."

"Oh, *that*." A.A. waved her hand. She knew everything about Ashley and Tri's breakup—Ashley had told her the whole thing, every boring detail. "That's ancient history."

"But I'm not sure you know the truth," Tri persisted.

"What do you mean?" A.A. couldn't face listening to this sorry saga again.

"The truth Ashley didn't want anyone to know," said Tri. He gazed down at his pants and picked at an imaginary thread.

"Know what?" asked A.A. impatiently.

"That the day after the . . . um, the Seven party, I went to see her."

"Yeah, I know all about that," she snapped. The last thing A.A. wanted to hear was how Tri went crawling back to Ashley on his knees, whining about how she was the only girl for him—just hours after he was kissing A.A.!

But Tri soldiered on with his story. "So I went to see her, and I told her that I'd kissed you, and that I thought it was best if she and I broke up."

A.A. did a double take. Say what?

"But she asked me if I would just keep pretending to be her boyfriend for a few more days. Until that whole *Preteen*

Queen thing was over. And I know it was really lame of me to say yes, but I felt guilty about kissing you, I guess. I thought that once the *Preteen Queen* party was over, I could ask you out. But then you were with Hunter so I kind of got mad at you, and then things have been all weird between us ever since."

"You told her about what happened at the Seven party?"

"Yup." Tri nodded, hanging his head. "She asked me not to say anything to you about our . . . our arrangement. I thought she didn't want to be humiliated, so I went along with it."

A.A.'s stunned mind was swinging faster than Ashley's trapeze. This was all news to her. According to Ashley, *she'd* broken up with Tri, not the other way around. She never said a word about knowing Tri had kissed A.A. Could all this be true? Had Ashley really lied to her?

"She never told me any of this." A.A. shook her head in disbelief.

"So now you know the truth." Tri gave her a hopeful smile. "I'm not telling you all this so you'll be mad at Ashley. I was just wondering—can we forget everything that's happened this semester and, um . . ." Tri blushed. "I mean, I think you know how much I like you."

A.A. glanced over at him. Tri's face was red, and he looked intensely nervous. How weird: This was *exactly* what she'd been hoping to hear from him this evening, but now that he was saying it, telling her he liked her, asking her out . . . it didn't feel right. It was all just too much to process.

On the one hand, Ashley had lied to her, so the whole time A.A. was annoyed with Tri, it was really unfair.

On the other hand, if Tri was such a pushover, giving in to Ashley's outrageous demands even though he knew it would hurt A.A.'s feelings, what kind of guy was *he*?

He must have seen how upset she was, how embarrassed she was when he never called her after they'd kissed. He did nothing, and then waited all this time to set the record straight. Was that what she wanted in a boyfriend—someone so indecisive and weak? Maybe they *were* better off just as friends.

"I don't know," A.A. told him, and that was the truth. She didn't know what to think or what to do.

She didn't know anything anymore.

33

MARIE ANTOINETTE WOULD
HAVE BEEN PROUD

ASHLEY STARED, BLINKED, AND THEN STARED
again. Was this really her cake? This giant
squashed ball that looked like it had been
picked up by a tornado, dumped somewhere in Kansas,
scooped up by a digger, and then bounced cross-country
back to her dining-room table?

Was that really supposed to be her, in miniature, cut in
half and waving forlornly from the top of the ball, looking as
though she was being swallowed alive by a giant half-sucked
piece of candy? And what were those gold strings hanging
everywhere—ropes or boogers?

"Sweetie, I don't know what happened," her mother was
saying, one arm around Ashley's trembling shoulders. "I'm
so sorry. We'll get you another cake next week, twice as big!

We'll have it sent to Miss Gamble's, so all the girls can have a slice. We'll get a cake so big it'll be included in the next *Guinness Book of World Records!*"

"It's okay, Mom," Ashley said. "I think I know what to do."

Lili had prepared her for the cake catastrophe, but Ashley had no idea it was this bad. She made up her mind quickly and walked over to the other side of the house, where the gaggle of ghouls were still laughing over their heinous breach of etiquette. Lili was right—they were a bunch of rebels without a clue. At least they had the decency to stop when they saw Ashley headed their way.

"Lili told me about the accident," Ashley said, a tense smile on her face. "But don't worry about it. I just want to make sure you guys have a good time."

They looked surprised at her reaction, and then one of the girls—the one with the unfortunate nose-pierce—piped up, "Yeah, this sucks. Is there anything else to eat around here?"

"Yeah, I'm hungry," one of the guys agreed.

"Of course," Ashley replied smoothly. "William," she said, calling on her butler. "Can you make sure these guests get more cake? You know, the one that was specially made?"

William raised his eyebrows, but he didn't protest. "Right this way."

Ashley watched them follow the butler and then dig into

plates of the "special" cake with a smile. Revenge is sweet.

What the horrid hangers-on didn't know was that the cake was special, all right. It was made especially for Princess Dahlia von Fluffsterhaus. They were eating dog food.

But Ashley didn't wallow in her victory for long. Something much more tragic was happening—the fact that she was about to turn thirteen at midnight and she was still NBK!

If only Cooper had come. Nobody else here counted. Well, that wasn't totally true—the other Ashleys counted. Of course they did. And her parents counted. They'd done everything they could to make her party a dream come true.

"And I'm really sorry I've been so distracted lately," said her mother, when Ashley had returned from her revenge errand. Matilda kissed the top of Ashley's head. "This new baby has been quite a shock for me and your father. For you, too, I know. And you've been such a little trooper!"

"I know," Ashley sniffed again. She really had been a trooper. Because her mother had been so out of it, all the responsibility for the party had fallen on Ashley's shoulders.

If it weren't for her dedication, everyone here tonight would be sitting at home feeling miserable and deprived, as though their lives were without meaning. Ashley had brought them so much happiness. And all she got in return was a no-show sort-of boyfriend and a trashed cake! Life was tragic, she supposed. Better get used to it now, before she was old and gray, i.e., twenty.

"Here are my girls!" Her dad rushed into the room, looking handsome in his sharp, well-cut suit, even if the only tie he could find read: ELVIS COSTELLO US TOUR '84.

He gathered up Ashley in his arms and squeezed her tight, crushing her. "Tildy, I think we should give Ashley her gift now, and not wait until later. To make up for this terrible cake fiasco."

"Yes!" Matilda's blue eyes widened, and she clasped Ashley's hands. "What a lovely idea! Are you ready, darling?"

"I guess." Ashley sighed, allowing herself to be led out of the dining room, through the lobby, and out the mansion's grand double doors. A crowd had already gathered on either side of the driveway, all cheering and clapping. But no Cooper. Why hadn't he come?

The gates swung open, and William—still in his lion suit—waved at her with a giant, furry paw. Then, to the oohs and aahs of the crowd, in roared a tiger-striped Vespa, driven by a guy in a black helmet.

Just what Ashley had wanted! She clapped her hands together and jumped up and down on the spot. Even though it wasn't the biggest surprise in the world, and even though she wasn't wearing her tight calfskin leather Vespa outfit as planned, she was happy. She hugged her father and gave her mother a big kiss.

"Here you are, darling." Matilda handed her the golden Vespa helmet that the Ashleys had given her as a prebirthday gift.

"Yay, Ashley!" cried Lili and Lauren in unison. They were both standing on the steps farther down, smiling proudly. Ashley waved to them and blew kisses, wondering why A.A. wasn't with them.

"But before you put it on," suggested her father, "maybe you want to get your other gift from the driver?"

Ashley scampered down the stairs, the Vespa helmet swinging from one arm. What was this other gift? A ticket to Rome, maybe? A bracelet with thirteen diamonds? A platinum Neiman Marcus card?

"Hello," she sang, beaming her widest smile at the Vespa driver. "I've come to ask for my other gift. What is it?"

The driver, dressed all in black, slowly pulled off his helmet. Ashley gasped.

It was Cooper!

But how? She looked over at her mom. "Did you have something to do with this?"

"Maybe." Matilda smiled. "Let's just say maybe some young gentleman came over the other day to RSVP personally for your party. He said it was important that you know he was going to be there."

Her mom was *sooo* cool. Ashley almost forgave her for having another child.

She turned to Cooper, who suddenly looked shy.

"Happy birthday, Ashley," he said, and leaned toward her. He was so handsome, she almost forgot to close her eyes. Her first kiss! It was even better than she'd hoped. It didn't even matter that there were a hundred people watching, or that the pesky Guinevere Parker was taking a digital picture, probably from an unflattering angle, to stick in the Miss Gamble's newspaper.

Cooper was here, helping her onto the Vespa, telling her to buckle on her helmet and hold on tight. She wrapped her arms around his waist and smiled to herself as he turned the scooter around and drove down the driveway, off into the night.

34

JUST CALL LAUREN
DR. FRANKENSTEIN

"BYE, ASHLEY!" LAUREN STOOD ON THE STEPS, waving, as the Vespa purred through the gates and into the street. It was kind of silly, waving good-bye to Ashley like this, when all she was going to do was turn around in five minutes and come straight back to the party. Cooper didn't look old enough to go anywhere but the end of the driveway. And anyway, the band still had another set to play. There was going to be a juggling contest at ten, and an acrobatics display at midnight. Ashley still had another two outfits to model.

Lili was instantly dragged off by her father to get her coat and say her farewells to the Spencers. Christian, who'd been standing behind them during the Vespa-giving ceremony, had loped off to get them ice-cream cones, so Lauren sat down on the broad stone steps to wait for him, hoping her shoeless feet weren't getting too dirty.

Not that Christian would care about something like that. She was so happy they were back together. She didn't even really mind the way Sadie had moved in on Alex right away. What did it matter, right? As long as Alex was happy, and Christian was happy, and she was happy, and Sadie was . . .

Hang on. Wasn't that Sadie sitting two steps away? And who was that guy she was leaning all over, giggling in a high-pitched, affected way that Lauren had never heard before?

It certainly wasn't Alex.

Lauren clambered to her feet and marched straight over.

"Sadie?" She looked from the blond bombshell to the beefy jock lolling next to her on the stairs. This was most definitely *not* Alex. "And sorry, your name is?"

"Todd," slurred the guy, winking at her. OMG! He had his hand on Sadie's knee!

"Would you excuse us for a second, Todd?" Lauren faked a smile and grabbed one of Sadie's perfectly manicured hands.

"Hey!" she protested, but Lauren continued to tug her first to her feet and then down the stairs. The gravel of the pathway dug into Lauren's bare feet, but it was too bad. She had some important business to deal with.

"What happened to Alex?" she hissed. Sadie pouted and rolled her eyes.

"He kept talking about you all the time," she whined. "I think he just wanted to come with me tonight to make you jealous. I don't really care. I dumped him five minutes ago, and it's no biggie—I already found another guy. Isn't Todd a doll?"

She looked back over her shoulder and made smoochy sounds in Todd's direction. Yuck!

"Who is he, anyway?" asked Lauren, almost grossed out by her behavior.

"He was here with that ho." Sadie pointed at a girl huddled by a potted bay tree, who looked like she was about to cry. "But I stole him right from under her nose. Pretty clever, huh?"

Lauren shook her head in despair.

"That's just mean," she said, frowning at Sadie's triumphant grin. "I don't get you. One minute you like Alex, and the next you're all over some other guy? Some other girl's boyfriend?"

"Don't be such a prude," Sadie snapped. She looked down her long, thin nose at Lauren, as though Lauren wasn't good enough to polish her Saint Laurent heels. "You said it yourself, earlier tonight. I look *amazing*. I *am* amazing. You're right. I shouldn't care what people think about me. And now I don't have to. Not when I look like this. It's all about *me* now!"

Lauren didn't know what to say. Sadie might look beautiful, but the way she was acting was plain ugly.

Lauren had groomed her to infiltrate the Ashleys, but she'd gone too far. Now Sadie was even worse than the Ashleys—mean, self-centered, fickle, and disloyal. Lauren's brilliant plan was a disaster, as spoiled as Ashley's birthday cake.

She'd created a monster.

EPILOGUES

Dear Diary,

All's well that ends well. At least between Christian and me. I like him so much, my head hurts thinking of what I put us through. He's so sweet and funny. I'm so glad it's just the two of us now. And Alex will be okay—at Ashley's party I saw him talking to some girl from Helena Academy who wasn't at all unattractive.

I'm a bit worried about the Sadie situation, however. On Monday she showed up at school looking très glam, even wearing knee-high boots with the uniform! You should have seen Ashley's face. She'd never thought of that. Then the very next day, Sheridan Riley, the girl who used to worship the Ashleys, turned up in the same exact pair of knee-high boots! So now Sadie and Sheridan are running around calling themselves "The S. Society." Looks like they mean to give the Ashleys a run for their money.

Things should get pretty interesting around here....

Warily,

Lauren Page

I've tried everything to get ahold of Max, but even though I'm off my electronic probation now, he won't take any of my calls, texts, or IMs. I can't believe he would listen to those Slytherin sluts over his girlfriend. There has to be something I can do!

You can't just break up with someone over a little misunderstanding, right? Over a silly thing like a camping trip? So what if I don't like to go camping and Max does? We have other things in common, don't we? Don't we? Why can't I think of anything?

For now, I'll just go log on his band's MySpace page again. He looks so cute in the video for their song "Uptight Girl." I wonder who inspired it?

Yours in mystification,

Lili

MEMO: FILE: DIARY: ALIOTO, ASHLEY
DON'T KNOW IF WHAT TRI SAID IS TRUE. IT'S
BEEN BUGGIN ME. RIGHT NOW ASHLEY IS
STILL MY BFF. TRI N ME R BACK 2 BEING
BFFS.
ALL IS BACK TO NORMAL, ☺
MAY-B I SHOULD ASK ASHLEY ABT WHAT TRI
TOLD ME?

I can't believe we still have to keep this stupid journal. Let's see. What is there to report? I have the most amazing boyfriend in the world. I couldn't ask for a better birthday gift. Or a better birthday.

Okay, so maybe after the party was over there was so much trash and glitter and debris all over the house that it looked like New Orleans after Mardi Gras and we had to spend the weekend at the Four Seasons just to get away from it all. It was still worth it, even if the tigers totally tore up the lawn and none of the staff who were shot out of the cannons will ever get their hearing back (which is why I'm so glad I found this dictation service).

Cooper was totally blown away by the whole extravaganza. That night he said he had something really, really important to tell me, but we got distracted when one of the fire-breathers came a little too close. By the time I finally shooed the guy away and asked Cooper what it was he wanted to say, he just smiled and said nothing.

That boy can be so maddeningly mysterious sometimes! Can you believe I still don't even know his last name? Oh well, maybe we should spend less time kissing and more time talking. Oh no—is this TMI? I think it is, so I'll sign off now!

ACKNOWLEDGMENTS

Thanks again to the fabulous Team Ashleys: Emily Meehan, Courtney Bongiolatti, Carolyn Pohmer, Paul Crichton, Matt Schwartz, Lucille Rettino, Richard Abate, Richie Kern, Melissa Myers, Paula Morris, Christina Green, and Adam Parks.

Love to everyone in my family, especially Mike & Mattie.

As always, big kisses to all my readers, who make writing the books worthwhile.

ABOUT THE AUTHOR

Melissa de la Cruz always expects to celebrate her birthday with hundreds of friends, glittering celebrities, and a seven-foot-tall cake with sparklers. She has yet to make her entrance on a trapeze, although she has made one on a Vespa, driven by a cute Italian model.

She has written many books for teens, including the bestselling series the Au Pairs, Angels on Sunset Boulevard, and Blue Bloods. She lives in Los Angeles with her husband and daughter.

Check out her website at www.melissa-delacruz.com and send her an e-mail at melissa@melissa-delacruz.com.